Summer Love
in
Music City

by
Joan Wahl

DEFIANCE PRESS
& PUBLISHING

SUMMER LOVE IN MUSIC CITY

Copyright © 2023 Joan Wahl
(Defiance Press & Publishing, LLC)

First Edition: 2023

DEFIANCE PRESS
& PUBLISHING

ISBN-13: 978-1-959677-81-9 (Paperback)
ISBN-13: 978-1-959677-80-2 (eBook)
ISBN-13: 978-1-959677-82-6 (Hardcover)

Published by Defiance Press & Publishing, LLC

Bulk orders of this book may be obtained by contacting Defiance Press & Publishing, LLC. www.defiancepress.com.

Public Relations Dept. – Defiance Press & Publishing, LLC
281-581-9300
pr@defiancepress.com

Defiance Press & Publishing, LLC
281-581-9300
info@defiancepress.com

Chapter One

⟊

S ummer couldn't quite describe why this birthday felt different than the previous ones. There were simply times when she felt like her life was being guided by an unseen hand.

When her twin sister, Autumn, and their college roommates, Bailey and Brennan, came to pick her up for her birthday celebration, they arrived in a limo. Before they were all even seated, she started peppering them with questions until Brennan finally stopped her and said, "You'll never guess, so don't even try."

When the limo started slowing down, signaling they had reached their destination, Summer was stunned. The arena marquee had flashing lights proclaiming that the evening's performance was sold out. "Oh my God! 'Martin Brody—Sold Out!' How did you manage to score tickets?"

"We won them," Brennan said with a smile. "Four front row seats."

Summer squirmed in her seat through the opening acts. When Martin Brody finally took the stage, there was a collective scream from all the females in the audience. After a ninety-minute show and two encores, he left the stage and left Summer sitting stunned in her seat, her eyes glazed over. She felt like a kid who had gone to the fair, eaten too much cotton candy, and gotten on the Tilt-A-Whirl.

The crowd started to disperse, and Summer and Autumn stood up to leave. "Let's give it a few minutes so we don't have to fight through the crowds to get to the exits," Bailey suggested.

"Good idea," Summer said and collapsed back into her seat.

A few minutes later, a security guard approached them. "Excuse me, ladies. I'm Andy. I couldn't help but notice you. I hope I'm not being too forward, but are you by any chance twins?"

They all thought it odd and Autumn, the most suspicious of the group, replied, "Why are you asking?" She inspected his security badge closely. It looked legitimate.

He leaned in closer and said in a hushed tone, "This isn't a well-known fact, because Martin likes to keep his private life private, but he has twin sisters. After a show, he sends a few of us out into the crowd to see if there are any twins. He always saves a few meet and greet passes in case there are."

Summer started to hyperventilate. "Did he say what I think he just said?" Suddenly energized, she leapt to her feet. "Let's go! Come on! Let's follow Andy." She followed the guard closely, like a puppy dog nipping at his heels, asking question after question. "Will he sign autographs? What about photo ops? Any special merchandise?"

"All your questions will be answered soon," he replied as he escorted them backstage. After posing for a few final photographs with fans, Martin turned and saw the four of them.

As he made his way toward their group, time stopped. Everyone else faded into the background until no one else was in the room except for him and Summer—then she saw him reaching out to hug her friends. "Bailey! Brennan! I'm so glad you could make it."

Martin turned toward her with his megawatt-bright smile. "I take it that these two neglected to tell you that I'm their big brother. My real name is Brody Martin." He took both her hands in his, and the electricity in the room increased a hundredfold. "And you have the most beautiful eyes I've ever seen."

"I–I know," she stammered. "I mean, I know who you are." He was still holding her hands. She was torn between wanting him to let go and wanting him to hold them forever. In that moment, the atmosphere changed so dramatically that later on, no one could describe what happened when their eyes met.

The silence was complete; no one wanted to break the spell. Finally, Bailey made the proper introductions.

"Ah, yes, the college roommates! I've heard so much about you."

"And yet we've heard nothing about you from these two," Autumn remarked.

"That would be all my fault. I have tried very hard to keep my family out of the spotlight."

"I'm … speechless." Summer managed to say as he continued to hold her hands in his.

"Trust me," Autumn said, "that's practically a miracle. Usually, she can't stop talking about you."

"Oh, stop teasing her," Bailey admonished. "Everyone we've introduced him to has been starstruck."

Starstruck? Summer thought to herself. No, it was more like being lovestruck. The conversation was still going on around her but she was having difficulty concentrating on anything anyone said. She had never seen eyes the color of his before. They reminded her of a tiger's, and she shivered as she thought about what it would be like to try to tame him.

Martin, aka Brody, suddenly realized he was still holding Summer's hands and took a step back. The loss of physical contact was like a blow to his heart. His reaction to Summer was like nothing he had ever experienced before.

"The twin thing was genius," Brennan said. "We had no idea how we were going to tell them we were going backstage."

Brody was every bit as distracted as Summer, but he nodded in agreement. All he wanted to do was usher everyone else out of the arena so he could be alone with her. She kept licking her soft pink lips, and all he could think about was wanting to taste them.

When it was time to move things along so the crew could break down the equipment, he didn't want Summer to leave. He hugged them all but held on to Summer for just a fraction longer. "I'll never forget this night," he whispered in her ear. The feeling of not wanting to let her out of his sight was unexpectedly strong, and a bit unsettling.

"Neither will I," she echoed as she felt his breath linger on her neck, setting off sparks.

Much to her surprise, her sister did not pester her the moment they were outside. Was it possible, Summer wondered, that she had only imagined the intensity of their connection? That no one else had felt the charged atmosphere in the room?

She didn't want to spend the ride home dissecting every aspect of the evening, so she feigned sleep until they were almost at her apartment. Plans were made for the following morning when they would get together to celebrate Autumn's birthday. Summer had been born just before midnight on the last day of summer, and Autumn shortly after midnight on the first day of fall. It had been nice when they were growing up because they each had their own day of celebration, but for the first time in her life, Summer did not want to see Autumn on her birthday. She just wanted to bask in the afterglow of having met Martin—*No, Brody*, she reminded herself—but she also knew if she begged off, she would never hear the end of it.

Sleep did not come easy that night. She kept turning over every moment in her mind. When their eyes met, she had been overcome with an emotion that was impossible to describe. If this was love at first sight, how was it possible that she felt it for this man? Someone who could never return her feelings? He was gorgeous, talented, and famous. He had dated actresses, models, even an Olympic athlete! He was eight years older and had a wealth more experience in all areas of life, especially when it came to love and romance. And yet, that did not stop her from weaving a "happily ever after" story in both her waking moments and her dreams.

When morning came, Autumn called to see if she wanted her to pick her up or meet them at their usual spot for a walk. "I could not fall asleep last night," Summer acknowledged. "Would you mind terribly if I met you at the café when you're ready for brunch? I promise I won't stand you up on your birthday."

Autumn grumbled a bit, as Summer predicted she would, but they arranged a time to meet at the Diamond Café.

Summer had just decided to try to get a little more sleep when there was a knock at her door. When she opened it, she found herself staring at the most beautiful bouquet of flowers she had ever seen. There were white roses, her favorite, and an array of other fragrant blossoms. Since the girl in the unit next door got flowers all the time, Summer figured they were obviously at the wrong apartment.

"Summer Reynolds?" The delivery man tried to position himself so he could see her past the extravagant display. "These are for you."

She couldn't imagine who they were from. She wasn't dating anyone—in fact, she hadn't dated anyone seriously in a few years. Even if a friend or her parents had sent flowers for her birthday, it wouldn't have been this glorious, undoubtedly expensive display.

She sat the arrangement on her kitchen table and was glad she was sitting down when she opened the card. *I never believed in love at first sight until you. Yours, Brody.*

Summer pinched herself. Surely, she was dreaming. Maybe the whole thing was a dream—there was no way this famous country star at the top of the charts felt the same way about her that she felt about him. That he had experienced the same out-of-body experience, the same rush of emotion, the same feeling of serendipity, of destiny.

She tried to get a little more sleep after calming herself down, but she did nothing but toss and turn. Finally giving up, she got ready to take a shower. Summer stuck her head in the kitchen, fully expecting it to be empty of the most impressive floral arrangement she had ever seen, but there it was. Still there, still real. She even read the card again because she could hardly believe what was written on it.

Before she made it all the way into her bathroom, her cell phone rang. Her heart raced with excitement and anticipation before she reminded herself that Brody did not have her cell number. She looked down and saw Brennan's name.

"Did you guys cut your walk short? Are you already at the café? I haven't showered or dressed yet."

There was a lot of chatter in the background. Summer could hear enough to determine that Autumn and Bailey were arguing.

Brennan sighed and said, "Your sister doesn't agree with what I'm about to do."

"Which is?"

"It seems our brother is as besotted with you as you are with him. He called wanting your phone number. Autumn thinks it's crazy. She doesn't—"

Brennan was cut off as Autumn grabbed the phone. "Autumn can speak for herself, thank you very much. This is crazy! He's a celebrity—a household name. Do you want to start down a road that can only lead to disappointment and heartbreak? Your heartbreak when he drops you for the latest Victoria's Secret model?"

Bailey was practically shouting in the background to be heard. "Our brother is not that shallow! A lot of stuff that has been written about his love life is greatly exaggerated."

Summer had heard enough. "Autumn, give Brennan back her phone. Now." She was usually fairly calm, but her temper was getting hotter by the second.

"Summer, I just—"

She cut her off. "I'm serious. Now." Her voice was getting louder, and Autumn reluctantly handed Brennan back her phone.

"So, what do you want me to do?" Brennan asked as though she hadn't heard the conversation between Autumn and Summer. "Have him call you, you call him? He did give me permission to give you his personal, unlisted phone number."

Summer was momentarily speechless. Was this really happening? Was she going to wake up any moment and find out it was all a dream? "You can give him my number, but it's hard for me to believe he is actually going to call."

"Oh, I don't think there's any doubt he'll call. He told me about the flowers."

Autumn could be heard in the background again. "Flowers? What flowers? You didn't say anything about flowers!"

Brennan just sighed. "I'll call him back and give him your number." Just before she hung up, Summer could still hear Autumn's protests.

Chapter Two

O nly moments later, her phone rang with a call from an unfamiliar number. "Hello?" she answered tentatively.

"Summer" was all he had to say for her to recognize his famous deep voice. "I hope the flowers arrived."

"You're beautiful." The words rushed out of her mind and her heart. "I mean, they're beautiful!" She felt like a teenage girl getting her first phone call from the boy she secretly liked.

"So are you." She heard his deep sigh. Was he as tongue-tied as she was? That hardly seemed possible. "I have to say, I'm not sure I've ever been at such a loss for words."

That made her laugh, which helped break the ice. "That's crazy! Your love songs are like poetry."

"Most people don't expect a guy to be a hopeless romantic, but I am," he admitted without a bit of shame. "Maybe it's due in part to having grown up with parents who are still best friends and madly in love. Now, I admit that when I was a teenager, it was a bit embarrassing to see them being so affectionate. But even back then I recognized that that was better than the alternative."

"Mine are the same way, which I am so grateful for. They have been great role models. I only plan to get married once."

"Me, too," he added quietly and thoughtfully, but changed the subject quickly. "Tell me about the rest of your family. Bailey and Brennan used to occasionally talk about you when you were in college, but I admit I didn't pay much attention at the time."

"My family dynamic is a lot like yours, minus, of course, having a superstar brother. My family also has female twins, and three boys. Autumn and I are the youngest, like Bailey and Brennan. My brother Shawn is twenty-five, Carter is twenty-seven, and Adam just turned thirty and is the only one who's married. He and his wife, Natalie, have an adorable daughter."

"The similarities are pretty amazing," he agreed. "I'll be thirty on my next birthday. I have one older brother, Blake, and one younger brother, Bryce. And oh, the stories I could tell you about how we all tormented Bailey and Brennan when they were young and we were all typical obnoxious older brothers. Frankly, I'm surprised they still speak to us! I do love my sisters, in spite of what they might have said about me."

She suddenly remembered where she had to be in an hour. "Speaking of sisters, today is Autumn's birthday, and I need to get ready to meet them for her birthday brunch."

"Can I call you later, before the show?" *Please say yes*, he said to himself. He wanted to know everything about her—her hopes, her dreams, her goals, and, most importantly, the status of her love life.

Summer was momentarily silent, hardly daring to believe this was really happening. But before she could respond, he spoke again, in a rush to get the words out, to ask the one question he so desperately needed an answer to.

"Before I go, though, I do have one important question to ask you." His voice had turned so serious, she could not imagine what it was he wanted to ask her. "Are you involved with anyone, either casually or seriously?"

"No," she was quick to answer, and he couldn't stop himself from breathing a huge sigh of relief. "And … since you were so eager to get my number, I'm assuming you are also unattached at the moment?"

"Unattached and available." That was what he said, although it was not strictly true. He already felt like she held his heart in the palm of her hand.

She was reluctant to say goodbye. "Where are you performing tonight?"

"Chicago tonight, then Minneapolis, and then Vegas. A lot of current country artists have performed there."

"And then?"

"A show in Toronto, then home to Nashville for a brief break before I head back out for the last leg of the tour."

She wanted to know what that meant for them, but she didn't want to ask just yet. Would he offer to travel to come see her? How would that work? It's not like he could take her out on a typical first date, and there was no way she would go to Nashville and stay with him. While she knew he was not quite as notorious a ladies' man as the press had painted him to be, at least *some* of what had been written about him was likely true.

"Have you ever performed in Vegas before?" She felt like she should know the answer to that question since she had followed his career for years, but her brain was so addled at the moment, she could barely remember her own name.

"No—and that reminds me, my parents are going to come to Vegas, and so are Bailey and Brennan. We actually have family there. I would never want to live in Vegas, but my aunt and uncle love it there." His nervousness growing, he was starting to ramble. He felt like the nerdy kid back in high school asking the head cheerleader to the prom. "What I'm trying to say—what I'm trying to ask is this: Would you like to come to the show in Vegas? Autumn is welcome to come, too, of course," he added, almost like an afterthought.

"How would we get there? That's only a week or so away." It wasn't like she could book a last-minute flight, even if it was within her budget to do so.

"I'm sending my plane." He said so matter-of-factly, it made her chuckle. "I'll actually be there a few days ahead of time to do a benefit concert for Tim and Faith's charity."

His plane. Tim and Faith. His world could not be more different than hers.

"This might sound a little silly, since I'm an adult living on my own, but I'm not quite sure what my parents would think. They don't even know who you are—well, of course they know who you are." Now she was the one starting to ramble. "What I mean is that they don't know you're Bailey and Brennan's brother and that we've met." *Or that I already can't picture my life without you*, she added silently.

"You might be surprised to know I lead a pretty normal life when I'm not on the road."

"Still, it's not like you can go to the grocery store or the laundromat without being mobbed."

"Okay, number one, it's easy to get your groceries delivered. And number two, I have a washer and a dryer. I know how to do laundry, and I know how to cook."

"So, you're the perfect man?" she teased, and then heard his sharp intake of breath.

"Far from perfect," he answered quietly. "But maybe, hopefully, perfect for you."

She had no immediate response to such a welcome but unexpected declaration. She was so quiet, he worried he had said too much too soon. They had, after all, just met, and they had not yet had a chance to spend any time alone together.

Finally, she responded. "You have no idea how much I would like to believe that."

"So … can I call you later? I can't say what time it might be, and I know you're a librarian, so I assume you have to work in the morning."

"I do have to work in the morning, but feel free to call later, regardless of the time." She was just as anxious to continue talking to him as he was to get to know her better, but she also knew Autumn would never forgive her if she didn't get her act together and get to the café.

"So, think about Vegas, and we'll talk later."

She could not bring herself to say goodbye, so instead she said, "Until tonight."

It was hard to get her head out of the clouds and her feet planted firmly on earth, but she somehow managed to get ready and only arrived at the café a few minutes late. Her sister and friends were already seated when the owner, Makayla, greeted her with a smile and a hug. "It's been too long. Happy belated birthday! The girls are at your usual table."

As Summer approached, you could have cut the tension with a knife. "No more talk about Brody today," she announced. "We're here to celebrate Autumn, and also hopefully to get her to tell us some of her wedding plans!"

The conversation turned to wedding talk as soon as they placed their orders. When Makayla brought their food over, Autumn complimented her on the change in décor, and Summer looked around in confusion. How had she not noticed the color changes, the local photos on the wall and the new flooring? They had been coming here for years.

While Autumn started talking about possible venues, Summer tried not to think about her future, and if Brody was really serious about what he had written on the card that came with the flowers.

For a time, Autumn ignored the faraway look in her sister's eyes and lack of attention to the conversation. But after a few minutes, she finally called her on it. "So, you actually think getting married while the entire wedding party is skydiving is a good idea?"

"What? Seriously? I know you and Dallas are adrenaline junkies, but that's just plain crazy."

"And not what I said!" Autumn struggled to keep her voice civil. "In fact, you haven't heard a single word I've said in the last five minutes, so why don't you just tell us about your conversation with Brody, assuming you had one, so we can move on to other topics?"

His sisters were dying to know if they had spoken but had not wanted to be the ones to bring it up.

"He called me. We're going to talk again later, after his show." She turned to look at Bailey and Brennan, knowing she could count on them to be on her side. "And ... he invited me to his Vegas show."

Before either Brennan or Bailey could respond, Autumn cut in. "Vegas? Really? After you've spent all of thirty minutes with him, none of which were alone? Mom and Dad will never go for it," she added, thinking that would be the end of the discussion.

Summer's voice was low but firm. "I don't care what you think. And I don't care if Mom and Dad approve or disapprove. I'm a grown woman completely capable of making my own decisions. I don't care if you think he's too old for me or if I'm too naïve; I don't care if you think I'm not good enough for him. I am going to see where this leads, and if it leads to heartbreak, then so be it."

"Sis ..." Autumn started, trying to smooth things over. "That's not it at all. I don't think he's good enough for *you*!"

Bailey responded in a voice of steel, "Be careful what you say about our brother."

"You know that's not what I meant," Autumn argued. "He's so much older in terms of experience that I just can't picture them being compatible in the long run."

"He invited you to go to Vegas, too, but if you can't put your feelings aside, I don't want you to go."

"I still say Mom and Dad will never agree to it." Autumn shook her head, so convinced she was right. "And how would you get there? Just impulsively buy a ticket and jump on a plane?" They all knew Summer was many things, but impulsive was not one of them.

"I'd be travelling with Brennan, Bailey, and their parents on his private plane."

"Private plane?!" Autumn exclaimed in disbelief. "Talk about a big sign about the differences in your lifestyles! Let's say, for the sake of argument, that you both want to explore your feelings for one another. How is that going to work? It's not like you can go on normal dates."

Summer did not mention that she had those same concerns; she didn't want to give her sister any more ammunition. "So, is your only problem his fame? Would you feel differently if he was just the older brother of Bailey and Brennan and he was an accountant or a lawyer?"

That stopped Autumn in her tracks as she tried to digest what her sister had just said. Yes, she was engaged, but was there some small part of her that was jealous of the attention her sister was getting? "I guess it is. Because otherwise, let's face it, he's totally …" She trailed off, not wanting to embarrass his sisters. "*Hot.*" She pretended to fan herself, and as the group laughed, the tension was broken.

"Agreed," Summer nodded, which made her wonder, not for the first time, what he saw in her. She was the quintessential girl next door.

The conversation then turned back to the birthday girl, and this time Summer gave her sister the attention she deserved. Regardless of how things turned out with Brody, her sister had always been her best friend and would be there for her no matter what. Autumn had never been the type to say "I told you so," and she wouldn't start now. Besides, Summer was truly happy for her twin and could not wait to help her plan her wedding. She would worry later about her parents' reaction to her news about Brody—and her intense reaction to him.

Chapter Three

❧

Much later that evening, her cell phone rang with the special ringtone she had chosen for him. "Hello, handsome."

"Hello, beautiful. I hope you enjoyed brunch with your sister and my sisters. Was there any talk about me?"

Summer could not help but laugh at his pitiful high school-like attempt to find out if he had been the main topic of conversation. "Some, but keep in mind my sister is newly engaged, so there was a lot of talk about weddings."

"What type of wedding do you want?" he could not help but ask.

"Hold on there, cowboy, let's take this one step at a time." She was somewhat alarmed to realize she was suddenly picturing him wearing his cowboy hat and nothing else.

"Okay, so, is the first step Vegas? I know you don't live at home anymore, but as I understand it, our parents did all meet one another when you and Autumn roomed with Bailey and Brennan your final year of college. Would it be helpful if my mother called your mother?"

"Is that sort of like your people calling my people?" she laughed. "No, the library closes tomorrow at five, so I'm going to talk to them in person. I feel like this is all going to be a little too unexpected to discuss over the phone."

"I take it you're quite close to them."

"I am, and I'm not ashamed to admit it."

"And you shouldn't be. I am very close to everyone in my family. We stick together, no matter what. When my parents brought Bailey and Brennan home after the accident—"

He stopped suddenly, unsure if Summer was aware that Bailey and Brennan had been adopted and were not his biological sisters.

"Relax," she said. "We've heard the story. I know their parents were close with your parents, and they adopted them when their parents died. They were only two, correct?"

"Yes, so they have no real memories of their parents. But the day they came home, they became my sisters, and I have never thought of them as anything but that." His voice was warm and sincere. "But getting back to Vegas. I don't want this to cause any issues between you and your parents. The last thing I want is to get off on the wrong foot with them."

"It will be hard to know how to approach the subject with them. For one thing, Autumn is not on board with this, and she thinks the possibility of a romance between you and I is totally unrealistic."

"Did you tell her it's not?"

"She wouldn't believe it even if you called her up and told her what you wrote on the card that came with the flowers."

"You didn't tell her?" he asked with a note of surprise.

"I wanted to just ..." *How to explain it?* she wondered. "Let it sink in a little more. To be honest, it all seems so sudden."

"But not unwelcome? Because I'll be totally honest with you. Yes, I want to spend time with you; yes, I want to get to know all about you, but my feelings are intensely personal and romantic and not in any way, shape, or form platonic. When you were about to leave the arena, I wanted to kiss you until we were both weak in the knees. I meant every word I wrote on that card. But if it will make your parents feel more comfortable about the idea, we will likely not have much time alone."

"Even though you want to kiss me senseless? And I want you to?"

"Even though."

"You have filled my head with all sorts of feelings I've never felt before." She needed to be as honest with him as he was being with her.

"I know you know about Elena and that we were engaged, but you have filled my head with all sorts of feelings I have never had before, either. When I looked in your eyes for the first time, it was like ... destiny. If I had felt that way about Elena, I would have married her."

How was it possible, she wondered, that everything he said so mirrored her own thoughts and feelings?

"Tell me more about Elena and the women before Elena. Well, the important ones."

"Elena and I were together for a little over two years. But to be honest, she never got over her ex-husband, and I always felt like something was missing. I think we stayed together longer than we should have because I had become so attached to her daughter, Raven."

How to ask this in a tactful manner? She struggled with trying to word it in a way that was not confrontational. "Have you had a lot of other serious relationships?" What she really wanted to know was how many women he had slept with, but she could not bring herself to ask that in such a direct manner.

"Not as many as the paparazzi would have you believe. I had a serious girlfriend in college. I was majoring in music therapy, and she was a music ed major. Sometimes on the weekends we'd go sing in some little out-of-the-way bar in Nashville. Strange as it sounds, that's how I was discovered. The guy who became my agent had come to town to see a band opening for a major tour and he wasn't impressed with them. He got lost on the way back to his hotel and happened to walk by the bar where Katie and I were singing, and he popped in."

"And the rest, as they say, is history?"

"Not quite. I did end up getting my degree online while I was working on my first record."

"And Katie?" She had never heard her name mentioned in connection with Brody's before.

"She wanted a normal life. Husband, kids, a job teaching music in a small-town elementary school."

Summer could not help but think that sounded a lot like her dreams of coming home from the library to her home, her husband, and her children. "And do you have any idea if she got everything she wanted?"

"She did, and we've kept in touch. Right before I had my first number one, she got married and asked me to sing at the wedding. She's still married to Brian. They have a cute little girl, Talia, and another baby on the way."

She thought it said a lot about his character that he and Katie were still in touch. "So, after Katie there was … ?" She hoped he didn't think she was being too inquisitive, but he had been linked with quite a lot of different women over the years.

He sighed. "I'm not proud of this, but my agent and my label head thought I needed someone glamorous to be my date to the first awards show where I was nominated for Male Artist of the Year."

Summer remembered watching that awards show on television and the hot model that had been hanging all over him, and hanging out of her skimpy outfit. She'd had some fancy name, like Bambi or Tiffany, and a body to die for.

"It was never a real relationship," he was quick to point out. "It was about being seen together at all the right places. Where, of course, our appearance would be mysteriously leaked to the press ahead of time so they could be there to snap our pictures."

"I remember her. She was hot with a capital *H*. You were a hot non-couple."

"You remember Peyton? How is that possible? *I* barely remember Peyton."

"You forget, I've been a fan since day one. I watched all the awards shows. And she was very … memorable."

"The word you're looking for is 'shallow.'"

"And skinny in all the right places, and well-endowed in all the right places."

The description was so spot-on that it made Brody laugh out loud. "But the girl never ate. Seriously. I don't know how she managed to survive. I'm quite sure she'd never had a burger or fries in her entire life."

"And who wants to live like that?" Summer laughed. "But really, you have to understand how intimidating it is to think about all the gorgeous women in your past. Was there anyone special after Katie and before Elena?"

"Some casual dates, but by then I was concentrating more on my career than my love life. And it's hard to maintain a relationship when you're on the road more than a hundred days a year."

"So, you're still on the road more than a hundred days a year. What does that mean for us? I mean ..." She backpedaled a little bit. "If we become an *us*."

"In my heart and mind, we're already an us," he said, wanting to reassure her. "But I know what you're thinking—the same thing everyone else is thinking. We've spent precious little time together, so how does that make us an *us*?"

"Exactly," she agreed. "And how can we accurately describe to anyone else what it was like the first time our eyes met? All I know is that every other man I date after you will never measure up."

"That's easy," he answered without a moment's hesitation. "Don't date other men. But are there any men in your past that I need to know about or worry about?"

"I had a semi-serious boyfriend, Paul, when I was in college. Autumn never liked him. I think she sensed something about him that I didn't."

He didn't like the quiver he heard in her voice. "He didn't ... take advantage of you, did he?"

"No. He cheated on me when I wouldn't sleep with him."

"What a loser. So, he didn't do anything to hurt you? I mean physically, because I'm sure that left some emotional scars."

"And I think that's why Autumn is worried about you and me. I think she thinks that in the long run, you and I aren't meant to last. Or that I won't be enough for you. Or that you won't wait for me."

He wasn't quite sure what she meant by that last comment. "I feel like I've waited my whole life for you. I began to give up on ever finding you. So, now that I've found you, what is it you think I'll need to wait for?"

"There is something you need to know." She took a deep breath. "I'm a virgin."

"So, by that, I'm assuming you want your first to also be your last?"

"Old-fashioned, I know, but yes."

"There's nothing wrong with being old-fashioned," he responded. "I will always treasure your feelings and your values. For the first time in years, I am wishing I was just the older brother of a friend. An architect or an engineer, someone who could take you out on proper dates. Someone who could court you in a traditional way."

It was hard to concentrate on anything he said after his comment about wanting to court her in a traditional way. Was it possible, she wondered, if deep down, he also had old-fashioned values? "You'll never be that guy."

He sighed. "I know, but I want to be *your* guy." His declaration was met with silence, and he wondered if he was starting to overwhelm her. "Too soon?"

"No, just too unbelievable. You could have any woman in the world. Why me?"

"Why *not* you? I know you're probably like a lot of other women your age. You've given some—or a lot—of consideration to the type of man you want to marry someday."

"True."

"But I bet you don't know that some guys also think about that stuff. And while I don't want to paint every model or actress with the same brush, I don't want to end up with someone who is beautiful but shallow, someone who just wants to be seen on the arm of a country music star. Like everyone else, all I want is someone to love me for me. Brody the man, not Brody the musician."

"So, what do you do when you're not on the road?"

"I'm a homebody. That doesn't play well with my supposed image, but it's the truth. I bought a log cabin-style home just outside of Nashville and spent the last two years fixing it up. Great views from the porch. I like to sit there and watch the stars come out."

"Are you the kind of guy every woman wants to find but that doesn't really exist? Like a magical unicorn?"

He burst out laughing. "No one has ever compared me to a magical unicorn. But when I'm not performing, I'm a pretty low-key guy who doesn't want a high-maintenance life partner. So, now that we've talked about what I want and don't want in a partner, what about you? What do you want and not want?"

"Nothing unrealistic. A partner, best friend, someone I can laugh and cry with." Now came the other topic she knew she had to bring up. She needed to get it out in the open before she spent any amount of time with him. "Back to my old-fashioned values for a minute … I do intend to save myself for marriage. And I don't mean until I have an engagement ring on my finger—I mean *after* the wedding. If that seems too unrealistic or hard to accept, it's best we both know that now."

His silence was unnerving. She was about to say that while she was flattered by his attention, she wasn't going to change who she was for anyone, including him, when he finally spoke. "If I tell you what I'm thinking, you might want to change your mind about me. About us."

"Try me. I feel like we need to get everything out in the open before we even think about the day when we might want to make our relationship public. Or do you think it's crazy to be thinking that far ahead?"

Here goes, he thought. He had never felt like he already knew someone so completely and so quickly at the same time. How could she possibly know that the idea of being both her first and her last was scary and sexy for him all at the same time? But he also knew that voicing that particular thought could be misinterpreted. "Everything you say makes me fall a little more in love with you. The sentiment on the card was from my heart. When I saw you that night after the show, I felt like my whole world shifted on its axis. I can't explain it any more simply than that. I looked into your eyes, and I just knew."

"I've never truly been in love, so it's hard for me to know what loves looks like. But I do know I want to spend time with you, and I do want to get to know you better to see if we ... click."

"Darling, if you're talking about chemistry, we have enough to blow up the science lab." His Southern drawl seemed more pronounced just then, and his words gave her goose bumps. "But if you're questioning if our initial connection could be real and lasting, it's okay. If you don't feel comfortable coming to Vegas, we'll figure something else out. I've gotten pretty good at hiding from the press when I need to. It's your call."

"My parents and my sister might try to talk me out of it, but my mind is made up. I'm coming to Vegas."

Chapter Four

The next day, Summer fretted about telling her parents about Brody and then fretted some more about whether it was even necessary. She had her own car, her own money, her own apartment, a full-time job, and was entirely self-supporting. Still, she knew she owed her parents a lot for her ability to be self-supporting. Thanks to their generosity and careful financial planning, she was not saddled with student loan debt like so many of her classmates. It was also true that she had never kept anything important from her parents, and she was not about to start now. Autumn was more of a mystery novel, while she was an open book.

Her parents were surprised, but pleased, that she was coming to visit them. They, too, were fretting about what a somewhat last-minute visit could possibly mean.

"Car trouble?" her father speculated, and her mother laughed.

"Scott, you're a wonderful father but a terrible mechanic, so I don't think it's that."

"Work problems?"

"Maybe she's having a hard time adjusting to living on her own for the first time? I know she and Autumn had planned to get a place together before Dallas proposed."

There was more back and forth until the door opened and Summer walked in.

"Honey!" Her father wrapped her in a bear hug. "It's wonderful to see you. Everything okay with the car?"

Much like her mother had, Summer laughed in response. "It's been a long day. Story time for the toddler group," she explained as her parents led her into the family room.

She had spent the entire car ride trying to decide how to broach the subject but, in the end, she just blurted it out. "I've met someone."

Her mother looked at her, confusion evident on her face.

"And that's great—isn't it?"

"It is. But he's someone ... famous."

"What do you mean by 'famous'?" Her mother was obviously wondering where on earth she would have met someone famous.

"It's Martin Brody." Once again, the words had rushed out of Summer's mouth before she could preface it with any sort of explanation.

"Martin Brody? The singer?" her father asked with a mixture of curiosity and disbelief.

Before they could begin to pepper her with questions, she said, "Okay, let's back up for a moment. His real name is Brody Martin, and he's Bailey and Brennan's brother. I met him after a show and we sort of hit it off. We've been talking on the phone."

"Isn't he a lot older? In his thirties?" her father asked, eyebrow raised.

"He's twenty-nine."

"And hasn't he been married?" her mother inquired not too politely.

"He was engaged. Once. She ended up reconciling with her ex-husband."

"But ... isn't he quite the ... ladies' man?" Summer could tell her mother was trying to be tactful but was failing miserably. The expression on her face said more than her words.

"I always thought so, too, but you can't believe everything you've read about him. Bailey and Brennan filled me in on what's true and what was blown all out of proportion. I think if you look underneath the public persona, he's a pretty regular guy. He's even still friends with his college girlfriend, Katie, and her husband."

Naturally, next they wondered why she was telling them all of this.

"He's invited me to see one of his shows in Las Vegas. Well," she was quick to point out, "he also invited Autumn to come along. His whole family is going, including Brennan and Bailey."

If anything, her parents now looked even more confused. "I know you've followed his career and listened to his music," her mother said slowly, her voice both strained and apprehensive, "but are you talking about wanting to date him?"

"Yes," Summer answered without hesitation. "I know how surreal this must seem. In all honesty, I'm still trying to wrap my head around the idea, too." She had no intention of revealing just how strong the connection had been from the very start. How she had taken one look at him and seen her future.

Her father tried to be careful with his words while still making a point. "After what you went through with Paul, we'd have concerns about anyone you wanted to date. And I know you've had the same concerns. But embarking on a relationship with someone so famous and recognizable will bring a whole other set of challenges. Do you think you're ready for that?"

Her mother also pointed out, though not unkindly, that he was years ahead of her in both age and life experience. "Have you thought about his life choices compared to yours? It's quite obvious he has been intimately involved with more women than just his previous fiancée."

Summer knew her parents would freak out if they knew she had already told him she was a virgin, so instead she said, "Don't worry, he knows I want to take things slow. And rest assured, I would feel the same way about anyone I was embarking on a new relationship with. Maybe I don't know what I'm getting myself into, but I do feel like I'll regret it someday if I don't at least spend some time to get to know him as a man, not the country music sensation."

Her parents exchanged a look that was difficult to discern. "So, tell us more about the Vegas trip," her father said, and she knew that was as close as they were going to get to fully giving her their permission. Not, she recognized, that she needed it—she just wanted it.

The discussion continued, and as the time grew later, Summer decided to spend the night rather than go home. It was both interesting and somewhat disheartening to realize that she felt differently about her apartment now than she had pre-Brody. While it was a cute little place, she didn't even have a plant that needed her daily attention. She was ready to have someone to share her life with, but she knew that hoping it would be Brody was unrealistic. Her head was telling her to be cautious, but her heart was telling her that he had already spoiled other men for her.

She spent the night in her old room, tossing and turning. She somehow felt years older than she had the last time she had slept in that bed, which had not been that long ago. Fortunately, the library did not open the next day until noon. She was normally an early riser, but since she had had a restless night, it was later than usual when she finally woke up and headed downstairs. Upon entering the kitchen, she found parents huddled around their coffee cups and whispering. As soon as they saw her, they stopped talking.

"What's wrong?" She could tell by the look on their faces that something had happened and that whatever it was, it wasn't good.

"Did you talk to Brody last night or this morning?" her mother wanted to know.

"No, why?"

Her father got up and hugged her. "You might want to sit down for this."

Now they were scaring her. "What's wrong? Was he in an accident?" Then an even worse thought struck her. Had his plane gone down? "Is he hurt, or ... ?" She could not even finish the question—she could not bring herself to ask if he was dead.

"Nothing like that. But this morning on one of the talk shows, they were showing clips from last night's show and the after-party. Apparently, he was seen with an old girlfriend. A *pregnant* old girlfriend," her mother added with a frown.

Summer did not react with shock or disbelief as they had expected. "Did they happen to mention the name of the pregnant ex-girlfriend, and was it Katie Bauer?"

"Yes!" her mother gasped. "Did you know about Katie?"

Summer tried to control her disappointment in the way her mother was reacting. "Do you honestly think I would start a relationship with not just this man, but any man who had fathered a child with a former girlfriend? If you had paid any attention to what I was telling you last night about Brody's background, you would remember me telling you about Katie, his college girlfriend. The one who is married now, with a young child and another one on the way. That he keeps in touch with her and is friends with her and her husband."

As if on cue, her cell phone rang with Brody's ringtone. Summer stalked out of the kitchen and went to take the call in the family room. As she walked off, she heard her father chiding her mother for thinking the worst of the situation. Summer was sorely disappointed in her mother's rush to judgment.

"Hey, handsome," Summer offered her usual greeting. "Just so you know, my parents are in the kitchen, debating the pros and cons of me dating you."

"I was afraid of this. I don't want to cause problems for you; I know you have a tight-knit family. And I have to say, if you were the star and I was the one entranced and had fallen quickly and completely, my mother would likely have the same reservations. Let's not be so quick to discount their reactions. I'm sure this came as a big surprise to them."

"I know you're right," Summer sighed. "But I didn't want to start out telling them about us and then have something like you being seen with Katie come up right away."

Brody tried to gauge how Summer felt about her parents' reaction. Was this going to change her mind about embarking on a relationship with him? Were they doomed to failure before they even began? He did not want to be the cause of a rift between her and her parents, and/ or her and her twin.

His silence troubled Summer. "What's going on in that gorgeous head of yours?"

"I don't want this to change how you feel."

"It hasn't. It won't. I'm ready for Vegas, and whatever comes next."

"I hope you are, because unfortunately the press can be brutal, and only a strong, solid relationship can withstand that kind of bullshit. It's the kind of thing that you can truly never be prepared for. Those initial weeks and months in the spotlight taught me that." He paused, not wanting to scare her off, but wanting her to think long and hard about what a relationship with him would mean—not just for now, but for the long run. "If you haven't already, you need to give that some serious thought. I've spent a lot of sleepless nights thinking about you—my life before you, what life would look like with you, and what life would be like without you. But you are the one who will be the most affected by whatever you decide."

"I've already decided. Not just about Vegas, but about all of it," she reassured him. "I know you well enough to know that even if there was an old girlfriend actually pregnant with your child, you would not abandon either one of them. I don't care what happened before me. I only care about what happens next."

Her words spoke directly to his heart. How was it, he wondered, that this caring, smart, sexy, yet innocent woman was the first one to understand him on this level? Understand his feelings, his morals, his lifestyle? "You can trust me when I say that there are no possibly pregnant former girlfriends that are going to come out of the woodwork. Elena was the last woman I was involved with."

That surprised her. He and Elena had ended their engagement close to two years ago. "So, no casual relationships since Elena?"

He answered slowly and sincerely, "No, and this might be hard to believe, given how the press makes me out to be the love-'em-and-leave-'em type, but I don't do casual. Ever since I ended things with Elena, I felt like I was waiting for something. For someone." He added silently, *I was waiting for you.*

A feeling very much like love washed over her in waves. "I didn't know what I was waiting for, either. Until you looked me in the eyes and took my hands in yours."

"Love at first sight?" he asked quietly. "Not just for me, but for you as well?"

"Yes," she whispered.

They said their goodbyes, his words stuck like glue in her brain. In the past, when something had seemed too good to be true, it generally was. It was so easy to get swept up in the romance of it and ignore the reality of it. There would always be numerous articles, photographs, and wild speculation about the latest woman he had been seen with. While part of her was thrilled that she could be the woman seen out in public with him, she had always been a private person. Did she want her entire life history and family and friends all put on display? How could they safely navigate the waters? Would they sink, or would they swim?

Chapter Five

The days flew by until it was time to leave for Vegas. The two continued to talk, sometimes twice a day. Summer had also received a phone call from Katie, who reassured her that the man Brody was today was really not all that different from the college boy she had known and loved. It was nice to be able to talk to someone besides his sisters about him.

In the end, Autumn had decided that a trip to Vegas on Brody's private plane would be too glamorous to pass up, and she assured Summer she was reserving judgment on their relationship until she spent more time with him.

Neither Summer nor Autumn had ever flown on such a small plane. Even though it seated twelve comfortably, they had only ever flown on large jet planes. It seemed both exciting and a little bit nerve-wracking at the same time.

Besides Bailey, Brennan, and their parents, they were also joined by one of Brody's brothers, Bryce, as Blake and his wife, Cassidy, had a young child and were unable to make the trip. Everyone was very welcoming, and both Summer and Autumn were struck by how unaffected they all seemed by their famous brother or son.

The plane ride was smooth, but Summer still declined all offers of food and beverages. Autumn was taking it all in without a care in the world, but for her, it was a just a trip to someplace she had never been before. Summer, on the other hand, was both quiet and uneasy. While she and Brody had agreed there were to be no public displays of affection, Summer still feared that the minute their eyes met, the chemistry would be undeniable and painfully obvious to anyone paying the least bit of attention. As far as the rest of the world was concerned, if anyone asked, she and Autumn were simply family friends, the college roommates of his sisters. Fortunately, the cover story was true and would hold up under scrutiny.

She also worried that perhaps they had both made too much of the original connection. Yes, they had spent countless hours on the phone talking about anything and everything, but she had not seen him once since the meet and greet. *What if this was just a fleeting thing?*

All her questions were answered when they departed the plane and two limos were waiting for them. As if by some prearrangement that she had not been privy to, everyone but Summer quickly piled into one of the limos. Autumn gave her sister a quick hug, pointed to the other limo, and said, "He's waiting for you. I'll see you at the hotel." And with that, the rest of the group drove off.

While she was standing there, both prepared and unprepared to be alone with him, one of the windows rolled down. From inside, he gave her a heart-melting smile. "You're even more beautiful than I remembered," he said, his voice husky with emotion.

She was flustered, excited and speechless all at once. The chauffer put her bags in the back and she joined Brody. For a moment there was silence, and then they both started talking at once.

"As exciting as this is, it's also still a little overwhelming," she admitted. "But … there's nowhere else on Earth I'd rather be."

"And there's no one else I would rather be with." He put his arm around her shoulder to pull her close. One of her questions was answered in that instant—she was fairly sure the electricity could have lit up the Vegas strip. "And I have a confession to make."

She smiled. "Me too. You go first."

"All I have been thinking about for the past thirteen days"—he glanced down at his watch—"ten hours and six minutes, give or take, is kissing you. Now it's your turn."

She turned her head so their lips were mere inches apart. "All I have been thinking about for the past thirteen days, ten hours, and six and a half minutes is kissing you."

"I knew there was a reason I told my mother to send everyone off in the other car." He leaned in to kiss her. The first kiss that he had meant to be sweet and slow was anything but. Her lips were molded to him in the most passionate kiss she had ever experienced, and when he slipped his tongue inside her mouth, her body responded instantly. Her nipples tightened as her body flooded with desire.

She took one of his hands and placed it over her rapidly beating heart. "I know we need to slow this down," she said with a ragged breath, "but this train is barreling down the tracks, and I don't want it to stop quite yet."

"I'm as overwhelmed as you are, but not surprised." She glanced down to see the evidence of his desire for her. "I knew it would be like this, with all those nights I was dreaming about kissing you, touching you, someday making love to you. But I don't want you to feel like I'm pressuring you in any way."

"What would you say if I told you I had those same dreams? That I wake up aching with desire and a feeling like nothing I have ever felt before? I've never felt anything close to this before, with anyone."

"Neither have I. I feel like we spent so much time on the phone that we've covered more things than some people who have dated for six months. I know all the little things about you, like your favorite color and your favorite flavor of ice cream, and all the big things, too, like your mother's miscarriage when you were away at camp, the name of the first boy you kissed, and the name of the first boy who broke your heart."

"Stop talking and kiss me again," she commanded.

He was more than happy to comply. They spent the rest of the ride snuggled up close, holding hands and talking in between both sweet and passionate kisses.

"Before we get there," he said, "we need to talk some about logistics. As much as I would like to walk around the venue holding your hand, we both know it's not a good idea. The press will be everywhere, and they'd figure out who you are in an instant and dig into your past, your family history, and speculate about our age difference and whether you are just the flavor of the week. Who are you? A groupie? A one-night stand? Not that I have ever had a one-night stand," he was quick to point out. "But you would not believe some of the stuff they would throw at you just to see what sticks."

He couldn't help but notice that she looked a little alarmed, as though she was suddenly wondering what she had gotten herself into. But when she didn't respond in either a negative or a positive fashion, he continued. "For now, it would be better to stick to the cover story. You're here with my family—you and Autumn were the college room-mates of my sisters. If anyone wants to check that, they will find out it's true, and that will hopefully be the end of their digging."

"I know you're right, but I do have one concern."

"If you only have one, you're better off than I am! What is it?"

"If they see us together, regardless of the setting or how many people we are surrounded by, don't you think someone will pick up on our … connection? The chemistry? I feel like fireworks go off every time you look at me."

He knew now was not the time to tell her what both her voice and her touch did to him. He felt like a horny teenage boy with an erection at the end of every phone call. Instead, he said, "Avoiding each other would probably make them more suspicious."

"Then you better not give me that look," she cautioned him.

"What look?" he asked, perfectly innocent.

"You know what look I'm talking about." He shook his head and she laughed. "The look you gave me when I got in the limo."

"And, I repeat, what look?"

"Like you hadn't eaten all day and I was dessert."

In spite of his better judgment, he leaned in and whispered in her ear, telling her exactly what he would like to do to her and with her when they were both naked and in a bed. He noticed she both blushed and smiled but did not look shocked. There were times he had to remind himself of her innocence, even though her response to his kisses told a different story.

"I'll try to control myself," he said. "But it will be hard."

She glanced down and laughed. "Good luck with that."

They arrived in the underground parking garage shortly after the other limo and everyone piled out, talking a mile a minute.

"I need to go rehearse," Brody advised them, "but you'll all have time to shower and eat and relax before tonight's show."

The large private elevator door opened and a well-dressed concierge walked out. "I'm here to accompany your guests to their suites, sir." He shook Brody's hand first and then turned to the group. "I'm Gregory, and I'll be available to you night and day during your stay with us."

Soon, they were whisked up to their penthouse suites while Brody took a different elevator to get to the concert venue. He dared not give Summer a kiss, although he knew that the staff would be fired if they were responsible for gossiping about their famous performers and their guests.

When Gregory opened the door to the two-bedroom suite that Summer and Autumn were sharing with Bailey and Brennan, there was utter and complete silence while they took in the glittering views. Even though Bailey and Brennan had stayed in lavish suites before in LA and Miami, nothing could compare to the opulence before them.

"Don't you feel like they made a mistake and put us in the wrong rooms?" Autumn whispered.

"Just think," Bailey commented. "If you married our brother, this could be your life!"

Autumn wasn't ready to jump on the Brody train quite yet. "A little premature, don't you think?" The other three looked at one another and shrugged, and she knew she was outnumbered.

They had several hours before the show was scheduled to begin, and while the rest of them were ready to explore the hotel and beyond, all Summer wanted to do was take a short nap. She had been so keyed up for days, she wanted to try to get some rest.

"We could always wait and go to the casino later, after the show,"

Autumn offered. They had all brought a small amount to gamble with.

The only gambling Summer wanted to do was with her heart. She all but pushed them out the door and as soon as her head hit the pillow, she was in dreamland—which, these days, mostly consisted of erotic dreams about Brody.

Later, when they were getting ready for the show, Gregory called to say he was on his way up with a delivery from Mr. Brody. It was still a bit strange to call him Brody when to the rest of the world, he was Martin Brody. Summer still expected to wake up someday from this long and glorious fantasy to find out that was all it had been.

None of them knew quite what to expect, but all Gregory did was hand a long, narrow black velvet box to Bailey when she opened the door for him. "This is for Miss Summer."

When Summer opened it, there was a collective gasp, then silence. There, nestled in the box, was the most gorgeous necklace any of them had ever seen. There was a small note inside that Summer read to herself.

"What?!" Autumn tried to grab it out of her hands. "Your first love note?"

"These remind me of the sparkle in your eyes," she read aloud.

"Holy …" Autumn trailed off, stunned. "Do you suppose they're real emeralds?"

"Oh, they're real. I handle all his insurance matters, and he asked me to add the necklace to his policy," Brennan added nonchalantly.

"Is your brother in the habit of buying expensive necklaces for the women in his life?" Autumn was both excited for her sister and concerned about whether it was normal for Brody to shower women with expensive things.

"He never has before." Brennan was adamant as she glared at Autumn before turning her attention to Summer. "He did ask me if I knew what color gown you were wearing tonight, and I made an educated guess."

Summer removed the necklace from the box with reverence and held it up to her neck. It fell in exactly the right place above the neckline of her shimmery green and silver gown.

"It's the most beautiful thing I've ever seen." She wished she could thank him in person, but she knew it was too big a risk to take. Blushing all the while as they all got ready, she took extra care with her appearance.

As they were escorted to their seats, the rest of the crowd watched and wondered who the lucky people were with seats in the very middle of the front row. Those tickets went for almost four hundred dollars each.

When Brody took the stage, he suddenly debated the wisdom of having them front and center. He had a hard time not looking directly at Summer, especially since she looked so beautiful and the necklace suited her so perfectly. Still, the shine of the emeralds paled in comparison to the glow of happiness in her eyes.

He performed all of his hits, some new songs he had sung at his last show, and then had a surprise announcement. "For my longtime fans here tonight, you all know that I am not normally one to talk about particular songs I have written, the story behind the song, so to speak. But this song, and the person I wrote it for, are very special to me. You could say that meeting her changed my life. So, I hope you are all ready for the world premiere of 'Summer Love.'"

The crowd cheered, but Summer was glued to her seat in shock. If his parents and his sisters were aware that he had written a love song for her, they had kept it to themselves.

Later, she could barely recall more than a phrase or two of the song. "*I hope my Summer love lasts forever*" and "*I see my future when I look in her eyes*" brought tears to her eyes, and she knew beyond a shadow of a doubt that every word he sang was true. Fortunately, many of the other women in the audience were similarly caught up in the romance of it, and no one paid her any particular attention.

When it came time to go backstage, Summer begged off. "If I go back there, everyone is going to figure out who I am. I wouldn't be able to stop myself from running up to him and throwing my arms around him. And you all know that I am not prone to public displays of affection." Her eyes glazed over with tears as she looked at her sister. She spoke softly so that no one could overhear, "He wrote a song for me. A *love* song. I never in a million years expected this. I wanted him to express how he was feeling, but I never expected him to express it to the world."

Even though Autumn was in love, and engaged, she was the practical one, the one who kept her emotions close, but this had overwhelmed even her. She reached out to hug her sister with tears in her eyes. "We all felt the love in that song. Just because it took me months to realize how I felt about Dallas doesn't mean love can't happen in an instant. I know he's a good singer, and a good songwriter, but that was a powerful song. You can tell the song came straight from his heart. Everyone in the audience felt it, even though no one knows he wrote it for you. About you."

"I hope he understands why I couldn't come backstage, even though I want to with every fiber of my being."

"I'll give him a hug for you. I'm sure he'll call when the meet and greet is over."

As Autumn and the rest of the group headed backstage, Summer started having second thoughts. She knew he would be disappointed to not see her, but would he understand? Would he take it as her having had a negative reaction to the song when all she really wanted to do was shout from the top of their penthouse suite that SHE was his Summer love?

In the end, she headed out with the rest of the crowd, hoping that since he had trusted her with his heart, she could trust him to understand how deeply the song had touched her.

Chapter Six

B rody was disappointed, but not completely surprised, that Summer did not accompany his family and Autumn backstage. He had known that not telling her about the song ahead of time was a risk, but he had wanted to surprise her, had wanted the world to know he had found the woman of his dreams.

When the only people left backstage were his bandmates, Autumn approached him first. She reached out to hug him and said in a voice filled with emotion, "The song was … moving. Beautiful. Perfect. There wasn't a single person in that audience tonight who would have any doubt you love my sister with all your heart."

His sisters and his parents had been similarly affected by the song and the sentiment behind it. When his mother hugged him, she asked in a hushed tone, "You've found the one, haven't you?"

He knew his mother had wondered if this day would ever come. While he had never been the playboy that the tabloids had made him out to be, he also had not had a long-lasting relationship since Elena, whom she had never entirely approved of.

"I have. She's it for me, Mom, even if it takes longer for her to feel the same."

"I saw the look in her eyes. You have nothing to worry about. I know she wanted to come backstage with us, but she was too overcome with emotion. She knew the minute you two laid eyes on each other that your secret relationship would be a secret no more."

He sighed. "We talked about this ahead of time. We were both afraid our connection would be too obvious. And, of course, she didn't know about the song. I debated telling her, but I wanted it to be a surprise."

"We were all surprised," his father joined in. "I see another number one hit in your future!"

"Her reaction is the only one that matters to me. I don't care if it never gets any airplay."

Bailey broke in, "I don't think you have to worry about that. Twitter is blowing up. Everyone is talking about 'Summer Love.' There are hundreds of fans already wanting to know when you're going to release a digital copy! I think it's safe to say this is going to be one of the biggest hits of your career."

His cell phone rang with a call from his agent, Evan. "I need to take this," he said as he stepped away for some privacy. "Were you able to make all the arrangements?" he asked. "Is everything all set?"

"Slow down, Brody," Evan chuckled. "Yes, everything is in place. But why didn't you tell me about this new song? The head of the record label already called me—they're already speculating about a possible Grammy nomination. I know that is one of the few things you have strived for that has so far eluded you."

Something even more important had eluded Brody all his life, but now he had found it. A life with Summer was the only thing he desperately wanted. If he never won a Grammy or was never crowned Entertainer of the Year, it didn't matter if she wasn't by his side.

Soon after, his family departed, and his band members went off to celebrate with their friends and family. He had been not-so-subtly trying to hurry them all along for the past fifteen minutes so he could call Summer.

She answered immediately, feeling like it had been days since she had seen him instead of only hours. All she could say was "Brody."

"My Summer love. I hope I didn't wake you up."

"There was no way I could fall asleep until we talked. I wish I could see you."

"So … the song was a hit?"

"How could it *not* be?" she inquired with amazement. "I can't wrap my head around you falling for someone so … so average—like me."

"Sweetheart, there is nothing average about you. You are the most beautiful thing I've ever seen. The necklace does not do justice to your eyes. You're sweet and sexy, and I love your smile and your spirit and your body." He lowered his voice to a husky whisper, even though there was no one around to overhear their conversation. "Especially your body."

Hearing him say that did things to her. "I want to see you," she said in a voice she hardly recognized as her own. "When can I see you?" While on one hand she knew they needed to be careful, the other part of her did not care who saw them together.

"I have an idea. Let me know if you need more time, but in about fifteen minutes, my agent, Evan, is going to knock on your door. He's forty-seven years old, about five foot eleven with shaggy brown hair and brown eyes."

"What should I wear?"

"If you're still in your dress from the show, that's great. If not, anything is fine."

"I'm still wearing it, mostly because I can't bring myself to take the necklace off."

Thoughts of her wearing nothing but the necklace flooded his mind. All the blood rushed to his groin. "Then leave it on. Evan will bring you here."

Evan arrived on time and drove her outside the city, where Brody was waiting in a vintage 1963 Corvette convertible.

"Great car," she acknowledged when she got in. "Is it yours?"

"Don't get too excited, it's a rental. And I wish I could put the top down, but I would be too recognizable."

"I love these cars."

He covered her hand with his. "I know. I remembered that."

"I'm amazed that a car like this is even available to rent!"

"You'd be even more amazed at the number of both classic and exotic cars you can rent in a place like Vegas. I could have rented a Rolls or a Jaguar or a Porsche."

She looked at him and grinned. "This car reminds me of you—flashy and sexy with more horsepower than I can handle. I'm drawn to your passion, your larger-than-life personality."

That worried him. He needed her to see behind the public persona to the man who was hopelessly in love with her. "I feel more passion for you than anything else in my life at this point. I love my career, but all I can think about is you. All I want is you."

She took his hand in hers. "And all I want is you. Okay, and maybe this car."

"One day I'll buy you one just like it, and everything else you have ever wanted."

"I repeat, all I want is you."

"And I'm all yours. But this isn't the only surprise tonight. Let's take a little ride."

She thought perhaps they were heading to the home of his aunt and uncle, where they could spend some time away from prying eyes. Instead, about thirty minutes later they pulled up in front of a small chapel and she looked at him, shock evident in her eyes. "Where are we?" This couldn't possibly be what she secretly hoped it was. She had been so anxious for Evan to deliver her to Brody, she hadn't noticed if the man was wearing a wedding ring. Maybe Evan was getting married and Brody was the best man. Maybe a fan had won a contest and Brody was singing at the wedding. Both of those scenarios made more sense than the one galloping through her brain and making her heart beat a hundred miles an hour.

"I'll explain in a minute, but I'd like to do it somewhere other than the car." He got out and, ever the gentleman, came around to open her door for her. Afterwards, she followed him inside.

The interior of the chapel was not at all what she had expected. There was none of the famous Vegas flash and glitter; instead, it was understated, filled with candles and vases of white roses.

She was about to ask if it was all for them when she turned and saw Evan and three strangers out of the corner of her eye. *Deep breath*, she told herself, *you're letting your fantasies run away with you*. But when she turned back around, Brody was down on one knee holding out a black velvet ring box.

Tears were shimmering in his eyes, and he looked terribly nervous. "I love you, and I want to give you my heart and my soul and my body and my name. But before you say anything, I need to tell you something."

"I don't care what that something is." Tears of joy filled her eyes. "Yes, yes, yes!"

"I haven't asked you yet," he reminded her, and she giggled. She felt like she was drunk on love. But when he stood back up, the ring box still closed, she was confused. "Aren't you going to propose?"

"I am, but first I need to explain something you deserve to know before you give me your answer."

What, she wondered, *could he possibly say that he thinks might change my mind?* She echoed his words, "I love you, and I want to give you my heart and my soul and my body."

"And that means everything to me."

"But?"

"But I want you to give me something that you aren't expecting, and that you maybe won't agree to."

"I'm completely confused."

"We've known each other less than two weeks, and while this feels very real and very perfect, I don't think anyone can be prepared for what it would be like to be married to someone as famous as I am. So, I'm asking you for a year. I want to marry you right here, right now, but I want us to wait a year before we consummate the marriage."

Thoughts she did not want to put into words flooded her brain. Was she to be put on the back burner while he was seen escorting other, more beautiful women around? Was he afraid she would be bad for his image? "So, what you're saying is you love me, but you're not attracted to me." She lowered her voice. "You don't want to have sex with me."

Before she could back away from him, he took her hands in his.

"Honey, we are not going to have sex—I am going to make love to you, and trust me, there's a big difference between the two. And yes, of course I want to make love to you. Every time I hear your voice on the phone, I feel like a horny fourteen-year-old boy who has to go masturbate in the shower."

Her eyes widened at the description and the visualization when he continued. "All I can think about is being inside you, about what it will be like the first time you give yourself to me. Your virginity isn't a gift you should give to me until you are totally and completely one hundred percent sure that you can live in my world. This is not about not wanting you—I want you more than anything I have ever wanted in my entire life. This is about loving you so much that I need to give you what you need, not what I need."

"So, am I understanding this correctly? We're going to get married and keep it a secret for a year? From everyone? My family? Your family?"

"Yes. I know this is hard to understand and even harder to believe, but marrying me is going to change your life in ways you can't imagine. So, I want to make you this promise. For the next twelve months, we'll spend time together. We can't go out on what you'd call regular dates, but I can promise you we will see each other at least every ten days. I'll make whatever arrangements I need to make. I know you have a full-time job, and I'll work around that and my touring schedule. You can come to my house, or my parents' house, or I can have Evan rent a house near you in his name and we can see each other there."

"You've given this a lot of thought."

"I have, and I know this isn't fair to you. I have no problem with going public with our relationship at some point, but I think we should wait at least six months."

"I understand all that, but why can't we make love? We'll be married, even if no one knows we're married. I'll know and you'll know and God will know."

"If you decide you love me but you can't live in my world, I want to be able to give you an annulment so you don't have to go through the pain and humiliation of a divorce."

"You're serious, aren't you?"

"I've never been more serious about anything in my life."

"So, at the end of the year, you'd let me walk away if that's what I want? And we'd never tell anyone we were married, and we'd get a quiet annulment?"

"As much as it would kill me, yes. Because even if I walked away from the music business tomorrow or a year from now, our life wouldn't change all that much. Fans would still approach me in a restaurant or a store or on the sidewalk."

She was stunned into near silence and disbelief. "You'd give it all up—for me."

"In a heartbeat."

There was nothing he could have said that would have made her more sure he was willing to give their marriage his all. How many men would be willing to give up their dream for the woman they loved? She couldn't imagine ever asking him to do that.

"Then tonight, I will give you my heart and my soul and the next twelve months. But Brody, you need to know one thing. Nothing will change my mind." They both knew she was naïve to think that, but neither of them said it.

He got back down on one knee and opened the ring box. "Summer Elaine Reynolds, will you do me the great honor of marrying me?"

"Is there anything else I need to know before I say yes?"

"Do you want children? Because I want children. But I don't want them raised on a tour bus, and I would never leave you home with them while I was on the road."

"So, would you want to wait awhile before we had them?"

"Only if you do. If you got pregnant on our wedding night—our *official* wedding night—I'd be the happiest and the luckiest man alive."

Her eyes sparkled like the beautiful pear-cut emerald ring as she nodded her agreement to everything, too overcome with emotion to speak. He placed the ring on her left hand and kissed her senseless. "If you'd rather have a traditional ring, a diamond engagement ring, we can exchange it."

"It's perfect," she said, voice filled with awe. "You're perfect."

Her eyes sparkled like the beautiful pear-cut emerald ring as she nodded her agreement to everything, too overcome with emotion to speak. He placed the ring on her left hand and kissed her knuckles. "If you'd rather have a traditional ring, a diamond engagement ring, we can exchange it."

"It's perfect," she said, voice choked with awe. "You're perfect."

Chapter Seven

van approached them and discreetly cleared his throat. They were so wrapped up in each other, they had not noticed his approach. "The officiant would like to know if you're ready."

Brody looked intently at Summer. "It's okay if you want to say no, or if you want to wait before making such a big decision."

She took his hands in hers and said with complete and utter conviction, "I will never change my mind. But I would like very much to change my name."

Evan, who had been dead set against this idea, couldn't help but feel that maybe he had been wrong. It had all been so sudden, and he had secretly wondered if she had some sort of agenda, but it was obvious she not been expecting a secret wedding. And even he had to admit that the love that shimmered between them was almost a tangible thing he could reach out and touch.

"Then let's get started," he said, handing Summer a small bouquet of white roses. "It would be my pleasure to escort you down the aisle."

"I accept," she said as Brody took his place by the officiant and the witnesses, whom she assumed were always on hand for short-notice ceremonies.

When it was time for them to recite their vows, Brody apologized to her and said, "I know you didn't have time to prepare anything, but before we recite the traditional vows, I have something to say." The officiant nodded at him and he began. "I bought your engagement ring the day after I met you. I flew to New York City and convinced Tiffany's to open early for me. I never thought I would give it to you this soon, but I knew it was meant to be yours, just as I am. I want to be your best friend, your lover, your husband, the father of your children. You are not the first woman I have loved, but you have my solemn vow that you will be the last."

Before the officiant began to ask Brody if he took this woman to be his wife, Summer spoke up. "I don't need time to think about what I want to say. This crazy whirlwind courtship of ours is like something out of a romance novel. Before I met you, if you had asked me if I believed in love at first sight, I would have said it was possible, but unlikely. But when I looked in your eyes, I knew I had found the other half of my heart. The one who would love me, laugh with me, and cry with me. I am not just giving you my heart; I am giving you my body, my purity, my virginity." If he was surprised that she had added that, he shouldn't have been. He knew she was proud of the gift she would give to only him. "I know you're not perfect, and neither am I. But I do think we are perfect for each other."

The officiant was aware she did not have a ring for Brody, nor did he have a wedding ring for her. They held hands as they recited the traditional vows, and when they were pronounced husband and wife and Brody touched his lips to hers, she thought she might faint. They had shared a lot of kisses in the past twenty-four hours—some sweet, some passionate, some quick, some long and lingering—but she would never forget this kiss. Their first kiss as husband and wife.

Evan surprised them with a small heart-shaped cake and two glasses of champagne. His toast was brief, but heartfelt.

After their mini celebration, Summer looked down at her beautiful ring. "I'm not sure you thought this through. I can't exactly go back to the hotel with an impressive emerald ring on my ring finger, even though it's not a traditional engagement ring. There would be questions."

Brody struck his forehead with a hand. "You're right, of course. I was so excited to give it to you that I didn't think any further ahead than that. I realize I gave you the matching emerald necklace, but a ring sends an entirely different message ... I'd hate for you to have to take it off." He hastened to add that it was already insured, if that changed her mind.

She slipped it off her finger, which already felt naked without it, and said, "I think it's for the best." After carefully handing it back to him, he slipped it back into the ring box.

"Would you like a different ring, one you could wear on your right hand? I would be happy to get you something a little less …"

"Glamorous? Expensive?" They both chuckled. "No, let's hold off on getting any other rings for now. Let's wait until we're officially engaged." They both laughed again. "It sounds funny to say that, considering we're already married. I wish I could shout from the rooftops that I am Mrs. Brody Martin!"

"I like the sound of that. So, let's make a promise to one another right now. One year from today, we will make it official."

"I promise."

"So do I." They sealed their promise with a kiss.

The rest of the night passed in a hazy blur of a dream. Fortunately, when she returned to the hotel, Autumn, Bailey and Brennan were all asleep. She knew she would have been unable to answer any probing questions, particularly from her twin, who somehow always seemed to know what she was thinking.

The next morning back at home, her parents were watching a morning show when the discussion turned to country music superstar Martin Brody.

"For those of you not privileged enough to have seen his sold out show last night in Vegas, here's a little clip for you. The music industry is all buzzing today about his new song, 'Summer Love.' I have some bad news for you single ladies out there—it would appear that Music City's most eligible bachelor is off the market! Speculation is rampant about who inspired the song."

Her parents looked at each other, too shocked and speechless to do anything but sit there and listen to a few verses of the song he had evidently written for their daughter.

"I have to admit," her mother said, shaking her head slightly, "I almost wish he had fallen for Autumn instead." Her husband gave her a questioning look. "Yes, I know full well that Autumn is engaged. But if she was available, I feel like she would not be quite so starstruck as her twin. Summer always has her head in the clouds, and Autumn's feet have always been firmly planted on the ground."

"There's no predicting love," her husband reminded her. "And we both knew when Summer fell, she would fall hard. I think our future son-in-law has captured her heart, and she has captured his as well."

"Future son-in-law? Do you really think it will get that serious?" Her mother sounded incredulous. *What would having a famous son-in-law be like?* she wondered. Fun? Crazy? Unpredictable? Probably all of the above and more.

"For some inexplicable reason, I do."

"Well, I think they will have a hard time getting to know one another on a deep enough level to make a lifetime commitment. He can't go anywhere without being recognized. And do we really want that kind of life for Summer?"

"It only matters if she wants it for herself," her husband answered wisely.

"If anyone finds out he wrote that song for Summer, she'll get thrown into the spotlight a lot sooner than either of them might want or expect. I just hope when she comes home from Vegas, she doesn't tell us they ran off to some chapel and got married by an Elvis impersonator!"

That made her husband laugh until his sides hurt. "I think the odds are better of one of us wining the state lottery. And we never play."

Summer had no idea that all the morning shows were talking about Brody, and the beautiful love song he had written for her.

On the other side of the country, Autumn sensed there was something different about Summer that morning when they got up. They all suspected, but did not know for certain, that when Summer had disappeared last night, she had been with Brody. Between spending time alone with him and the song, Autumn had expected her sister to be on cloud nine. Instead, she seemed moody.

When they went to the home of Brody's aunt and uncle for brunch, she thought that Summer and Brody seemed somewhat distant with one another, whereas she had expected their starry-eyed looks to grate on everyone's nerves. When Brody announced he needed to leave early for his show in Toronto, she wondered if there was trouble in paradise, but she wisely kept her thoughts to herself.

It continued a few days after they returned home, and Autumn finally called Bailey and Brennan to see if they could shed any light on what had transpired after the show. "Did Brody say anything to either of you?" she asked, ready to kick his ass if he had broken her sister's heart.

"Not a word. We're as mystified as you are as to why they were behaving the way they were at brunch. Maybe you should just show up on her doorstep unannounced and find out what's going on. If she tries to make some kind of excuse, tell her you're there to talk about wedding stuff, then change the subject." They all knew Autumn was the master of subterfuge.

Autumn checked the library's schedule on their website and showed up at Summer's apartment at 10:30 a.m. the next day, knowing she could not use work as an excuse since the library did not open until 1:00 p.m.

When she heard the doorbell, Summer hoped that it was Brody, even though she knew he would never just show up without advance notice. She was not at all surprised to see her sister, however, since she knew she had picked up on her moodiness. But it wasn't like Summer could just tell her she was missing her husband.

She opened the door and ushered her sister inside. "Come on in and let's get this over with."

As soon as they were seated, Autumn jumped right in. "You haven't been yourself since the morning after the concert. I'm assuming this has something to do with Brody." She had not phrased it as a question, but Summer nodded her head nonetheless. Autumn took a deep breath, knowing she was making an assumption, but she had to ask. "Did he—or is he—trying to push you into a physical relationship? I can't fathom what else might've happened. The two of you barely made eye contact at brunch. Even Brennan and Bailey picked up on it!"

Summer knew if she blurted out the whole truth, Brody would be furious. So, she thought frantically, what else could she say to throw her off track?

"We had a long, hard talk about what it would be like to go public with our relationship this soon. I was all for it; he was not. He thinks I need more time to, as he put it, weigh the pros and cons of what a relationship with him would be like in the long run. It's not like I fell in love with some average guy. I'll basically have to share him with thousands and thousands of fans."

"He's not wrong about that, "Autumn agreed, impressed with Brody's thought process. "Being in love with a celebrity means being exposed to all kinds of things. Articles in the tabloids, speculation about who he was photographed with when it's anyone other than you. You've always been more private of a person than I am. Can you live in a fishbowl like that?"

Summer knew she was right, but it irked her anyway. "It's not like I'm involved with someone running for president and they're going to do a full background check on me. At this point, all that really matters to me is that I love him and he loves me."

Autumn knew her sister had her head in the sand, and she also knew she had a habit of being incredibly obstinate when she dug her heels in. "But what happens if the day comes when he doesn't? Your heartbreak would be on display for the whole world to see. And that would break my heart."

"And it would break *my* heart to not even try," Summer said quietly but firmly.

Autumn, however, wasn't ready to drop the subject yet. "Have you made any sort of plans about how you are going to accomplish spending time together? Or is this all some abstract thing, both of you think-ing it will all just fall into place? And have you thought about the fact that at some point, he is going to want to be intimate with you? Maybe sooner rather than later?"

As much as she hated to give away even this much information, she went ahead and told her sister he knew she was still a virgin.

Autumn looked both shocked and somewhat pleased that the subject had already been brought up. "And he's okay with that?"

"He doesn't really have a choice. He knows I'm adamant about not having sex with anyone until I'm married." If Autumn knew that Brody was, in fact, willing to give her an entire year to be sure of the strength of their love, she would be totally and completely on his side.

Autumn knew she couldn't continue to push her sister and risk alien-ating her, so she decided it was time to have a little bit of fun with her. "Did you know that Mom and Dad thought you might come back from Vegas married by some Elvis impersonator?" Summer burst out laugh-ing. *There was no Elvis impersonator there*, she thought to herself.

"Like I would ever get married without you and Mom and Dad and Adam, Carter, and Shawn there."

"I know," Autumn agreed. "I told her it was a crazy idea!"

Summer looked at her watch. "I have time for lunch. Let's go to Rudy's and get some burgers and fries." Mentioning burgers and fries reminded her of her conversation with Brody about models. It seemed everything these days reminded her of Brody, or of some conversation they'd had.

Lunch with Autumn went smoothly without another round of twenty questions, for which Summer was grateful. She was seriously question-ing how she was ever going to keep their secret under wraps until there was an engagement announcement. She wanted to spend Christmas Eve wrapped up in his arms in front of a fireplace. She wanted to ring in the New Year in his bed. She wanted to celebrate his birthday and Valentine's Day, which were only a day apart, in some romantic tropical location. And if, heaven forbid, they didn't end up staying married, how could any other man ever compete with his memory?

She knew she was destined to love Brody forever, even if their marriage didn't last that long.

Chapter Eight

❧

As hard as it was for her to compartmentalize everything in the following days, she knew she needed to do it, or else she'd face more questions she didn't want to—or couldn't—answer. It was turning out to be challenging to find time to talk to Brody in private without having to worry about being overheard. They were also fast approaching the deadline he had set for making every effort to see her every ten days, and she wondered if he had been serious about that after all.

One night when he didn't have a show and the library had closed right at 5:00 p.m., they had more time for a long overdue in-depth conversation.

"Any special plans this weekend?" he asked, and she sighed with what sounded like regret.

"The library is closing early this Friday for some routine maintenance, and I'm supposed to go dress shopping with Autumn and my mother. Do you have any idea how hard it's going to be to watch my sister try on wedding gowns when all I can think about is wanting to try them on myself?" She realized she sounded envious, but then that was exactly what she was. "But I don't have any plans other than that, and believe me, I'd get out of it if I thought I could."

"Can I send Evan to pick you up Saturday morning around nine? I want to spend the day with you."

"I'm in!" she happily agreed. "Care to give me any hints? What should I wear?"

"Keep it casual. Comfy clothes—jeans, hoodie, sneakers."

"Am I allowed to tell anyone we'll be together?" Not that she saw any need to do so; after all, she would only be a call away.

"Sure, but not where."

"Well, since you haven't told me where we're going, that won't be a problem!" They spent the next hour catching up on the events of the past few days, and when they hung up, she started counting the hours until she would see him in person.

The evening spent dress shopping with her mother and Autumn was sheer torture, but Summer put on a happy face and tried very hard not to stare longingly at several dresses that caught her eye. Autumn didn't find anything that suited her, but Summer had made mental notes about several gowns she herself liked.

She spent a restless night, and when Evan came to pick her up, she was relieved to find he was friendly and chatty. She had been worried things might be awkward. When she got into the car, he leaned over and said, "Nice to see you, Mrs. Martin."

"It's nice to hear someone besides Brody call me Mrs. Martin." She wondered if she could get him to spill the beans about the day's plans. "Do you have any idea what we're doing?"

"No, I don't know what he has planned. I think he wants it to be a surprise."

She chuckled. "Nothing could be nearly as surprising as our impromptu wedding."

"Agreed. I'm not sure how much you know about his early days in the business, before he had his first number one. Did you know I was the one who discovered him?"

"Yes, he told me about the sheer coincidence of you walking into that tiny little bar and hearing him singing with Katie."

"Not many people have heard that story. For one thing, back when it all first started, Katie wanted no part of it, and he didn't want to make things difficult for her. And I can't really describe what it was like to walk in there and hear his voice for the first time. I know he didn't think I was on the level when I told him I wanted to sit down with them the next day. While I had fully expected to sign a new duo to the record label, I was perfectly happy to sign just Brody."

The rest of the ride was spent with Evan regaling her with stories of Brody back in what he referred to as "the early days." "The thing

I like the best about Brody is that he's still the same man today. He's matured, and his voice has matured, but he's still the same down-to-earth guy next door. His fame and his fortune have not changed him."

They pulled into a small airstrip and she saw Brody standing next to the same plane they had travelled to Vegas in. Summer literally leapt out of the car and into his waiting arms. She hadn't even thought about who might be within listening distance when she leaned up and whispered in his ear, "Hello, husband."

"Hello wife," he said before wrapping her in a passionate embrace, unconcerned that Evan was watching.

He introduced her to the pilot, one of two that flew for him regularly, and said there would be no one else on the plane except for the two of them. "Didn't want any distractions. Or questions." He reached into his pocket, pulled out her engagement ring, and slipped it on her finger. "I wish you never had to take this off again."

"I know. But for now, it's enough to know I can wear it whenever we're together."

He was suddenly struck with the vision of her wearing her engagement ring and nothing else, and his body hardened in response. Before he could make a move he knew he would regret, the pilot announced they needed to get buckled in for takeoff.

"Are you going to finally tell me where we're going?" she asked with a smile as they taxied down the runway of the small airport.

"I want to show you my home. I don't want you to feel like we have to live there," he was quick to point out. "It's a great house, but if you want to buy a different house, that's fine. I know we need to make it our home. I just want to get a feel for what type of house you like."

The plane ride was short and smooth, and when they landed, one of Evan's vehicles was there waiting for them. "I borrowed a car in case you wanted to see some of the sights before we head to the house. No one will recognize me in Evan's Jeep with the tinted windows."

Thinking about seeing the house made her nervous, but she decided she would rather head directly there than check out downtown Nashville. To keep her nerves in check, she started asking him a million questions. But there was one thing she was especially curious about. "Is the place where Evan discovered you still open?"

"Sadly, no. I think it's something like a dry cleaner's now. But I have to tell you, the place really wasn't much to see, even back in the day."

The incessant questions and comments continued until he started to laugh. It was obvious she had done some research about his city. "It sounds like you already know a lot about Nashville."

"I'm sure there's a lot you could teach me." The comment was innocent but ripe with sexual innuendo, and she blushed endearingly when she realized how it sounded. "I just meant—"

"You're adorable. I know what you meant, and someday, we will have all the time in the world for lessons. Both in and out of the bedroom."

Before she could think of a response, he pulled up to a gated driveway entrance and punched in a security code. The long winding driveway led to them a beautiful, sprawling log cabin-style home that took her breath away. "It's beautiful, and the setting is perfect. It's like the house is part of the surroundings!"

He was amazed to hear her echo his exact reaction from when he had seen the property for the first time. "That's why I bought it. That and the two-story great room with a towering stone fireplace."

She had already fallen in love with the house, and she hadn't even been inside yet. But as they approached the front door, she hesitated. Before he turned the key, he looked at her troubled green eyes and could read the questions that clouded them. He took both her hands in his and answered her silent questions. "I have never brought another woman here, and I have certainly not slept with anyone here. I bought the bed for the master suite when I bought the house."

"You know me so well," she whispered, more to herself than to him. As she held her breath in anticipation, he opened the door. Directly across from the entryway was the great room with the soaring fireplace and windows so high and clear, she felt like she could see for miles. "What a great place for a Christmas tree."

"I haven't had a tree since I bought the house. Sometimes I'm on the road until the twenty-first or twenty-second or I leave right after the first of the year. Never seemed worth the effort." He pulled her in and held her close. Even the scent of her shampoo was intoxicating. "This year, and every year from now on, you're going to help me pick out and decorate a tree." He kissed her sweetly. "I'll give you the grand tour."

The house was beautiful, but at the same time it had the look of a place well loved. There were family photos everywhere, potted plants on the kitchen windowsill, sheet music on the grand piano. The kitchen was something out of a magazine, and she wondered if he really enjoyed cooking or if his mother had helped him pick out the appliances and cookware.

"I know you said you like to cook. Were you serious, or is all this just for show?" She couldn't help teasing him a bit.

"When I'm not on tour, I actually enjoy cooking. But trust me when I say this: I was a much better student in my grandmother's cooking school than either of my sisters. I swear Brennan can barely boil water, and once Bailey almost burned down the kitchen."

He next led her to the media room, where he showed her a collection of movies he had picked out especially for her. "I made sure to have all your favorites. Later, we'll watch one and make popcorn." She was touched by the fact that he was trying hard to make the day seem like the kind she would share with a regular guy, someone who wasn't a household name.

"What's next?"

"Let's go upstairs."

"Why, Mr. Martin," she said flirtatiously. "What kind of a lady do you think I am?"

"The kind of lady I have been waiting for my entire life. You have no idea just how arousing and intimidating it is to know I will be your first."

"And my last," she reminded him. "I guess I get the arousing part, but intimidating? It's not like I have any basis for comparison."

"I'm going to want to make it last, but I'm afraid I'll be too excited to control myself."

He led her into the master suite and she perched on the edge of the bed. "So," she said slowly and seductively, "I make you want to lose control?"

He could see where this was heading and pulled her up. "I am not going to lose control of this situation today, as much as I would like to." The bedroom was spacious and lovely without being overly masculine. But the thing she was the most impressed with were the side-by-side walk-in closets.

"I've had *bedrooms* that weren't as big as these closets!"

"We'll fill the bedrooms with love and making babies, and you can fill that closet with everything your heart desires."

She looked deep into his eyes so he could both hear and see her sincerity. "The only thing my heart desires is you. I love you, and I love your house. I want to live here and sleep next to you and make babies in this bed."

"We better go back downstairs, because if you keep looking at me like that, I'll begin to seriously rethink the whole celibacy thing."

"When you look at me like that, I feel it from the top of my head to the bottom of my feet, but mostly somewhere in between." She kissed him so passionately, he thought he was going to spontaneously combust.

"Come on." He took her by the hand. "Let's go downstairs. I'll make a fire, and you can pick out a movie."

It was all too easy to sit back on the comfy leather sofa beside him and get a glimpse into what their life together could be like when he wasn't on the road. When the movie was over, they talked more about their childhoods, their families and friends, and she gave him her perspective on what it was like to be a twin. "Autumn and I are so different in both appearance and personality. Your sisters seem so similar, whereas Autumn and I are like night and day. That made for some interesting experiences growing up. Most people find it hard to believe we're twins."

"You have to admit, you don't look that much alike."

"Maybe that's a good thing, or you might have fallen for my sister instead. And she is already spoken for!"

"Not a chance." He shook his head. "When I first looked in your eyes, I swear my heart stopped. It didn't start beating again until I took your hands in mine and I thought … 'This is the kind of love people write songs about.' And while I have written love songs before, I had never written a song for someone I was in love with."

"I still can't believe you wrote a song for me. A song that, as I understand it, people in the music industry are already referring to as your career song! Possibly your first Grammy-nominated song."

"I don't care if it never wins any awards. And if you don't want me to perform it in my live shows, I won't. All I could think about when I was writing the song was what a great story it was going to be to tell our children someday."

"Do you want to put it on your next album?"

"Only if you want me to."

"I do. I want everyone in the world to hear it. How soon will you be putting your next release out?"

"I have other things on my mind right now, other priorities. My wife is at the top of that list. No, scratch that—my wife is the *only* thing on that list."

"But what about your tour?"

"We're wrapping it up earlier than usual this year. My band has been begging for time off between Thanksgiving and New Year's, and we scheduled the tour accordingly. Our last date is the week before

Thanksgiving, and we don't go back out until mid-January. Oh!" He suddenly remembered something very important. "Will you be my date for New Year's Eve? There's something I have always wanted to do."

"Me too," she admitted, looking at him expectantly. "What are the chances …"

"Ball Drop in Times Square?" they both said simultaneously.

"Yes!" She practically jumped up in glee. "But … you can't be in that crowd. How would that work? You can't exactly go incognito. And it's too soon for us to be seen in public." She didn't feel that way, but she knew he did.

"All that's true. But how would you feel about watching it from a rooftop garden?"

"You own a place in New York City?"

"No, but a friend does. He'll be in Paris for his honeymoon, and he offered it to me. And, not to worry—it has a master suite and three bedrooms."

He could see the wheels turning in her mind, and he had to admit his thoughts were taking the same route. Directly to one of the bedrooms.

When it was time to fly her back home, they were both reluctant to see their day together end, and she was equally reluctant to take her engagement ring back off. The only thing that cheered her up was knowing they would be spending both Thanksgiving and Christmas together, and then they were going to ring in the New Year together. Grinning to herself, she committed to making sure they made some fireworks of their own.

Chapter Nine

The following weekend, Summer approached her parents about the possibility of spending the Thanksgiving holiday with Brody and his family. She knew it would be a hard sell, and naturally, it was. Her mother was concerned that her relationship with Brody was moving too fast, while her father was taking more of a "wait and see" attitude. In the end, her parents agreed that they would go to Tennessee for Thanksgiving, and Autumn and her brothers could join them if they chose to.

When the day before Thanksgiving arrived, Summer, Autumn, their parents, and their brother Shawn and his girlfriend, Kyra, all piled into the family SUV to make the trip. Her other two brothers had made plans of their own, and Summer was secretly just as glad that her entire family wasn't going to descend on Brody all at once.

Summer had been concerned that the three-hour drive was going to be filled with endless questions by her mother, but for the most part, she behaved. Summer was glad when the conversation turned to Autumn's fiancé, Dallas, and his reasons for not joining them. Summer was secretly concerned there was trouble in paradise, but she kept her thoughts to herself.

The guest house was a delight, and the room Summer had selected for herself and Autumn to share was filled with white roses. Other lovely bouquets filled the other two guest rooms.

"He's trying too hard," she overheard her mother whisper to her father. "How did he know what my favorite flower was?" Her father just laughed and said that he was happy to see Brody had done his research.

When they walked outside to go to the main house, the pathway was lit with luminaries. From there, they could see the great room windows were graced with the sixteen-foot-tall Christmas tree Summer had helped him select.

"Wow" was all her mother could manage to say. "Does anyone else feel like we stepped onto the set of that old television show, *Lifestyles of the Rich and Famous*?" It was hard to tell if she was impressed or thought it all a bit too much.

"Brody's a pretty down-to-earth guy," she reminded her mother. "If you take his fame out of the equation, they're just a normal family. They've had highs and lows like everyone else. Brody doesn't flaunt his wealth or his success; his parents still live in the same house he grew up in. He did buy vehicles for his sisters, but his brothers are both successful and self-supporting."

Brody's parents, Lynn and Mitch, opened the door and welcomed the Reynolds family like they were lifelong friends, even though they had only met Summer's parents briefly when their daughters were in college.

It took all the willpower Brody had to not wrap Summer in a heated, passionate embrace. Somehow, he managed to restrain himself and offered her a brief kiss instead. They knew all eyes were on them, and their love was shining more brightly than the fire in the fireplace.

"Welcome to my home, Shawn, Kyra, Mr. and Mrs. Reynolds."

"Please call us Leslie and Scott." Summer's father reached out to shake Brody's hand, and Brody gave her mother a quick hug. She had not thought to warn him that her mother was not very touchy-feely, but Summer thought her mother seemed pleased rather than annoyed. *Score one for Brody,* she secretly thought. He also reached out to hug Autumn.

"The tree is lovely," she said. "How tall is it?"

"Just over sixteen feet. And, you'll notice, it is not decorated yet. One of our long-standing family traditions is to decorate the tree the day after Thanksgiving, so I'm pleased that you're all staying until Saturday and will be able to join us!"

Summer's father turned to her and said, "I brought something for Lynn and Mitch, but I left it in the guest house. Maybe you and Brody could run over and pick it up. It's in the bag next to my suitcase." He gave her a sly wink.

Summer and Brody didn't hesitate before they were holding hands and practically racing over to the guest house, eager to take advantage of a moment alone. As soon as they were inside, she was in his arms.

"Remind me to thank your father later," Brody said before he dipped his head and kissed her with all the pent-up passion of the past eleven days. "You look beautiful, and I love your sweater. It's the exact same shade as your eyes." His hands lightly caressed the soft fabric over her breasts, and he heard her sharp intake of breath. "What is this fabric?"

"It's angora."

"You look like an angel," he said, his breath ragged as the devil on his shoulder wanted nothing more than to peel that sweater off her and get a taste of her breasts. "I wish I could kiss you everywhere I want to kiss you." He gave her featherlight kisses on her forehead, her nose, and each perfect little ear. "We better get back before they send your sister or your brother or your mother here to fetch us. I can tell your mother is the one I need to win over. Your father seems a little more receptive to our relationship."

Summer reached over to pick up the bag. "And I better get the gift before we leave without it. Your kisses scramble my brain and make it hard to breathe."

"At dinner tomorrow when it's my turn to say what I'm thankful for, I want to say what's on my mind and in my heart, but I know it might be too much too soon. So, I want to tell you now, while we're alone. Over the years I have had many, many things to be thankful for, but I have never been as thankful for anything as I am for you. I've never been a particularly religious person, but I feel like a higher power led us to one another. If your friends Erica and Hannah hadn't transferred to another college, you wouldn't have roomed with my sisters. Maybe you would have met them at some point, especially with them also being twins, but maybe not. Then you wouldn't have come to my show with them. Right now, you would be dating someone else, and I would have spent the rest of my life searching for you."

His impassioned speech brought tears to her eyes, and they quickly threatened to spill over. "I was meant for you, and you were meant for me. We would have found each other, one way or another."

As they began their walk back to the main house, much slower than their race to the guest house had been, he stopped her. "There's one more thing I need to say. I wish more than anything that I could give you your engagement ring tonight. I want to see it on your finger—I want everyone to know we are together for life. But I know it's too soon, and I don't want any resistance from your parents. They need to get to know me. They need to see us together so they know this is real. I need to show them, with words and actions, that you are the most important thing in my life."

His words were so heartfelt, so real, so touching. Summer hoped with all her heart that at the end of this visit, her mother would realize that she was not just a passing fancy of Brody's, but instead someone he had real and deep feelings for.

The meal and the rest of the evening seemed to pass effortlessly. Family stories were shared, and aside from the similarities of having raised twin girls, it turned out the Reynolds family and the Martin family shared many similar interests. After dinner, their parents decided to take advantage of the warm weather and went outside to sample some of Mitch's homemade wine by the firepit. All in all, it had been a successful evening, and Summer was thrilled. In spite of the fact that she was a grown, self-supporting woman, she still valued the opinion of her parents very highly. It was one of the things Brody found most appealing about her.

When morning arrived, so had the rest of Brody's family. Bryce and his girlfriend, Charlotte, had arrived late the night before, and then Blake and his wife, Cassidy, arrived with their adorable three-year-old daughter, Madelyn, who instantly stole Summer's heart.

Leslie and Lynn shooed Summer out of the kitchen and told her Brody was waiting to take her for a walk around the property. She was anxious to see what progress he had made on his home recording studio.

"I didn't think we'd have so much time alone together," Summer admitted happily. "Everyone, including my mother, has been so accommodating."

When they were out of sight of the main house, he stopped to take her in his arms. "I want to kiss you again and scramble your brain." He proceeded to do exactly that, kissing her until she was weak in the knees and her body responded with a now familiar ache.

She pressed close against him to feel him harden in response. "I wish you could feel the effect you have on me, but there really are no words ..."

"So, my kisses make you speechless?"

"I was going to say aroused." She blushed and he chuckled at the sweet, sexy admission. "I wonder how we're possibly going to wait to consummate our marriage until our official wedding night. I swear I spend half my time thinking about what it's going to be like between us."

"Wonderful." He kissed the side of her neck. "Exciting." He teased her nipples until they were tight little buds. "Indescribable." He cupped her rear until there was no space between them.

"You're making this really hard for me."

"Ditto," he whispered, and she glanced down at the proof of his desire. "Now, come on. Let's head for the recording studio before I decide to run back into the kitchen, tell everyone we're already married, and whisk you off in my private jet to a deserted island."

His crew had made great progress on the recording studio since the last time she had seen it. "I'm a desperate man," he admitted. "By the time we're ready to go public, I want to have this completed. I know you won't want to move in before we are officially married, but I'd love it if you spent as much time here as possible."

In that moment, they were both painfully aware that every conversation seemed to revolve around how she was going to fit into his life. She was the one who would have to leave her apartment, her job, the life she had made for herself. As much as she loved him, she was at times worried about losing too much of herself. But now was not the time to bring that up.

"Come on, husband, let's head back to the house before I decide to run in there, tell everyone we're married, and drive to the nearest hotel. I wouldn't be able to wait to get to the deserted island to have you make love to me!"

He sighed and stood up. "You're right. Let's get back to the house and see what we can do to help out in the kitchen."

She giggled. "I wonder what your fans would think if they saw you in an apron?"

"Not going to happen." He shook his head, but she just grinned.

When they got back to the house, the kitchen was in a state of controlled chaos. "Too many cooks in the kitchen!" Brody's mother acknowledged. "I shooed everyone out so Leslie and I could get to know each other better. Autumn and Kyra are setting the table and Cassidy, Bailey, Brennan, and Charlie are in the great room getting the ornaments out for our tree-trimming party tomorrow."

"Sounds like things are well in hand. Did you save any jobs for us?" Brody asked.

"Please say yes," Summer pleaded. "I want to see him in an apron. That would be a great photo op!" Everyone, including Brody, laughed.

"Here," Lynn said. "You can wear mine, Brody."

"Oh, no, if I'm going to wear one, then Summer needs to wear one, too."

"Done," Leslie replied, untying her apron. "Here's mine. Now we just need your phones so we can take pictures of both of you."

They had fun posing for silly pictures with a turkey baster and a whisk that Brody held up like a microphone. When he tried to convince Summer to sing with him, she distracted him by reaching into a bag of flour and flinging some onto him.

He retaliated by sprinkling some flour in her hair. Before she could reach for more, he pulled her in for a kiss and his mother snapped another picture. "Dinner is almost ready." Lynn was trying very hard to look stern, but failed miserably. "Go get cleaned up and call everyone to the table."

As soon as Summer and Brody left the kitchen, their mothers turned and looked at each other. "I'm not quite sure what to make of all this," Leslie admitted. "I've never seen my daughter act so giddy and care-free before. But seeing Brody here, surrounded by his family, gives me a better glimpse into the life of the man my daughter has fallen in love with. It's just so surreal for all of us. She's been such a big fan of his for so many years that it's hard to separate the two parts of his life."

Lynn patted her hand. "If it helps, I've never seen my son so wrapped up in someone. I don't know what the future holds for them, but I will tell you this: He wants a home, a wife, a family. He has a five-year plan in place that involves stepping back from touring as often and concen-trating on songwriting. He would never be the kind of husband to leave his wife and children behind while he tours nonstop."

Leslie nodded tentatively, still skeptical. "When Summer gives her heart, it will be forever."

"And I know the reason that Brody did not marry Elena was because he knew deep inside that something important was missing from their relationship. He never looked at Elena the way he looks at Summer. They have to find their own way, of course … but Mitch and I would be thrilled to have Summer for a daughter-in-law."

"I'm not quite there yet, I have to be honest," Leslie replied with a dry chuckle. "But I hope you know my hesitation is more about the suddenness of this, and has nothing to do with Brody personally."

"I'd feel exactly the same way if I were her mother," Lynn reassured her. "Now, let's go round up everyone to help us take all the food into the dining room."

Chapter Ten

The feast was truly a work of art. The food was set up buffet style, and Summer and Autumn were pleased to see a few of their family's traditional Thanksgiving dishes had been included.

After everyone had their plates heaping full, Lynn reminded everyone to save room for pie. "We have apple, pumpkin, and pecan."

"Sometimes we have leftover pie for breakfast," Brennan confided to their guests in a whisper loud enough for everyone at the table to hear. "Then we all decorate the tree. We've been doing that for as long as I can remember. We spend the whole weekend together as a family."

Scott squeezed Leslie's hand under the table. "Sounds like he comes from a pretty great family. I don't know about you, but they're winning me over."

"As hard as it is for me to admit," Leslie replied softly, "I have to agree."

As the two families lingered over the meal, the conversation flowed easily and everyone took turns telling stories and sharing memories of holidays past.

Everyone had just agreed they needed a break between dinner and dessert when Lynn said, "Don't forget—it's time for my favorite Thanksgiving tradition!" Her children groaned, but she continued anyway. "Every year," she explained, "we go around the table and everyone says what they are most thankful for this year." Her eyes sparkled with mischief as they landed on her middle son. "I think Brody should go first."

Since he had already poured his heart out to Summer, he did not want to overemphasize how much meeting her had changed his life for the better. "I'm thankful that Bailey and Brennan went to the same college as Summer and Autumn and that they ended up as roommates."

Brennan pointed her finger at him warningly. "You should be thankful we didn't tell them stories about what a terror you were and how you treated your twin sisters when we were four or five and you were twelve or thirteen!"

"That's true," Brody admitted with a laugh. "I'm thankful for that, too."

As Summer waited anxiously for her turn, she considered what to say, glad she did not have to go next.

When it was Blake's turn, he glanced at his wife and she gave him an almost imperceptible nod. "We're thankful for all of you. And we're especially thankful to live close to you, Mom, since we're hoping you can help us out with your next grandchild, who is due in early April."

Pandemonium ensued, and there was an outpouring of laughter, hugs, and more than a few tears. Brody felt equal amounts of joy and envy. He could not wait to see his child growing inside his wife.

As all the talk of babies subsided, it was time to return to the thankful game. When Summer's turn came, all eyes were on her, waiting to see what she was going to say. Her mother in particular looked both curious and worried.

Finally, she said, "I'm thankful for Evan. If he hadn't discovered Brody singing in that tiny club, the world would have been deprived of Brody's voice."

She had no way of knowing that she could hardly have said anything that would have touched Brody more. That day had changed his life, which in turn changed hers some years later.

The rest of the family continued with the thankful game, with some offering up serious thanks and some more silly. All in all, it amazed Summer to think that they all seemed so comfortable around one another. It was like they had all been close friends for years.

Several hours later, after everyone had stuffed themselves with pie, Summer and her family returned to the guest house with a plan to return in the morning for breakfast pie and tree decorating.

Autumn excused herself to call Dallas in private, and Summer said she was going to go soak in the tub. Her mother gave her a look, but Summer continued before she had a chance to speak. "I know you and Dad want to pick apart everything Brody and I said and did, so go ahead and have the discussion without me. I know how I feel about him, and I know how he feels about me. The rest of you just need to catch up."

Shawn felt the need to jump to his sister's defense, as he had many times since she had been born. In many ways, he was closer to her than he was to his brothers. "I think we need to leave them alone and let them figure things out for themselves. I know it's hard to wrap your head around Summer dating a famous musician, but I have to say, I was very impressed with him tonight. And his family seems pretty great, too."

It seemed like everyone was in agreement except their mother, but Summer knew better than to push it. Their mother was more stubborn than the rest of the family put together.

Summer counted herself fortunate that she wasn't subjected to a lengthy play-by-play of how everyone thought the evening had gone. She was surprised, but grateful, that both Autumn and her mother left her alone with her thoughts.

When morning came, it dawned beautifully with just a bit of a chill in the air. As they entered the main house, they were welcomed by a flood of wonderful scents coming from the kitchen.

Shawn took one look at the breakfast spread and complained, "What, no pie? You promised me pie for breakfast! That apple pie was the best I've ever had."

"Thank you," Brody said. "I made that one from scratch." He took some good-natured kidding, but it was true.

Kyra had a cinnamon roll in her hand and hesitated before taking a bite of it. "You need to marry him, Summer. We need a baker in the family. I know you were all counting on me, but I'm hopeless in the kitchen." When Shawn agreed with her, she punched him good-naturedly in the arm. They had lived together for several years, and while they acknowledged they were going to get married eventually, they were in no hurry. And Shawn, in particular, did not want to steal the spotlight from Autumn, having no idea that there was going to be another family wedding.

"Brody was a much better kitchen apprentice than either Blake or Bryce," Lynn said. "As for Bailey and Brennan, they were beyond hopeless."

After feasting on quiche, breakfast potatoes, fresh fruit, cinnamon rolls, and even leftover pie, to Shawn's delight, it was time to decorate the tree. Brody and his father had already strung the lights, and Mitch and Blake were in charge of decorating the top branches.

It was a big job, but with so many people helping they made short work of it, with Lynn or Mitch stopping from time to time to share a story about a special ornament.

Summer selected a photo ornament of a beautiful young girl, seeing it was neither Bailey nor Brennan. She turned the ornament toward Brody's parents and asked innocently, "Who's this?"

Lynn had forgotten that was still in the box of photo ornaments, and she looked slightly nervous. "That's Raven. She's—"

Summer interrupted, "Elena's daughter, right? She's beautiful." If anyone was surprised that she knew who Raven was, they didn't acknowledge it.

When the tree was done, the Reynolds family admitted they were still far too full to have lunch, and it was about time for them to head for home. Before they left for the guest house, Brody took her parents aside.

"I realize that this is a holiday weekend, but if you have no objection, I'd like Summer to stay for another day or two. My family would like to spend more time with her, and I would drive her home, of course."

Her father answered before her mother could think of a reason to say no. He was impressed that Brody has asked them if she could stay, rather than just assuming they would not mind. "Of course!" He shook Brody's hand. "Just bring our girl back safely."

"You have my word, sir. And Mrs. Reynolds, rest assured that my parents and sisters will be here the entire time."

"Call me Leslie," she reminded him, and then she shocked everyone by reaching out to hug him. "I know she'll be in good hands. Thank you for inviting us into your home. It was a lovely holiday."

Her warm tone both pleased and surprised him. "I hope it's the first of many."

Tears shone in her eyes. His sincerity had touched her heart. "So do I."

Summer had had no idea that Brody was going to ask her to stay, and while both she and Brody knew she did not need her parents' approval or permission, it was a meaningful gesture.

Shortly after her family left, Brody whisked Summer away without telling her his plans. Somehow, she was not surprised when they arrived at a small airport to find his familiar plane waiting for them.

"Where are we going? Are we spending the night somewhere? You rushed me out of the house so fast, I don't have anything with me but my purse."

"While I would like nothing better than to spend the whole night with you, I told your parents that my parents would be around. This is just a day trip. While we were watching one of your favorite movies, I had a brainstorm."

"And are you going to let me in on it?"

"It's a surprise."

"You are the king of surprises, after all. Although I'm sure you know that no surprise is ever going to come close to the surprise wedding."

He reached into his pocket and handed Summer her engagement ring. "I could not wait another day to make you mine," he said. "I admit, I was petrified that you would meet and fall in love with someone else and forget all about me."

She thought it endearing that he actually believed someone else could have turned her head when her every waking moment since the time they had met was filled with nothing but thoughts of him.

As they talked and held hands, she began to not care or even wonder where they were heading. They were together, and that was all that mattered.

When they started approaching their destination, the pilot came on and said, "Sir, if you and Miss Reynolds look out to your right, you'll see the hotel. It's a lovely view from the air."

It wasn't just any hotel they were flying over—it was the Grand Hotel on Mackinac Island, where one of her favorite movies had been filmed. "It's beautiful!" she gasped with delight. "I wish we could tour it. What a lovely surprise!" They were so in tune, he knew her thoughts and desires almost as well as she knew them herself.

"That's only part of the surprise. The hotel is closed for the season, and they won't open until May. But I wondered if perhaps that's where you'd like to get married? I truly could not think of a more romantic location."

Her eyes were overflowing—she was too touched to speak. All she could do was nod her head. "It's perfect," she finally managed to say, her voice weak. "And I know we can't make any actual plans until we announce our engagement, but I wish I could start looking at wedding gowns," she said wistfully.

"When is your sister's big day?"

"July first. My parents will have time to recover from that before we get married."

"I'd offer to pay for our wedding," Brody said, "if I thought that wouldn't offend your father." Before she could interrupt, he continued. "Keep in mind that we'll need to think about things that your sister and Dallas won't need to worry about. We won't want the location leaked to the press. We'll have to think about how we want to handle formal photographs, if we think we will need security there. And, if we do decide to get married at the Grand Hotel, we will have to book the entire hotel to ensure there won't be anyone there that wasn't invited." Summer was starting to look worried. "But the advantage of getting married there is that no vehicles are allowed on the island."

"Maybe we should elope so we don't have to worry about any of that." She had spent a great deal of time thinking about what it might be like to be married to someone so famous, but not so much the actual ceremony details.

"No," he said, insistent. "We are going to have a proper ceremony— a beautiful, romantic ceremony. You deserve nothing less. Plus, we have months to figure things out."

Chapter Eleven

The weeks between Thanksgiving and Christmas passed by quickly even though Summer and Brody had only managed one quick get-together before he headed to her hometown on the twenty-third in anticipation of Christmas. She was surprised when he had shown up unannounced on the eighteenth, explaining that he and Evan had been in a town about an hour from her scouting out a location for a possible show in the spring.

The morning of the twenty-third, it started to snow, and Summer started to fret about the weather. Autumn was off for the holiday, and the sisters were spending the day together wrapping gifts.

Every five or so minutes, Summer got up to look out the window and complained incessantly about the weather. "I hope Brody doesn't have any trouble flying in this afternoon," she commented for about the fifteenth time.

"I'm pretty sure he'll get here by dog sled if he has to. Besides, hasn't he had the same pilots and the same plane for a number of years?" Summer nodded in response. "I'm sure they are used to flying in all sorts of weather."

Summer had started daydreaming when Autumn brought her out of it suddenly. "Have you thought about whether you and Brody are heading down the aisle?"

Summer almost choked on her tea. "What prompted *that* question?"

"I've seen the way he looks at you, and you're walking around on air. I know it's only been three months, but you can't tell me it hasn't crossed your mind."

Summer knew her sister would question a denial. She had no choice but to answer as honestly as she could. "Of course I've thought about it. He's everything I've ever wanted in a man."

"Do you think you know him well enough to be certain of that? And even if you are, have you given any serious thought to what that future would look like?"

Summer went back to standing at the window, afraid her sister would see all the secrets hiding behind her eyes. "There are a lot of things to consider. Would I want to go on the road with him, for example? It's not like I could continue working at the library."

"Or anywhere, for that matter," Autumn said wisely. "Are you worried that if you become Mrs. Brody Martin, you'll lose sight of Summer Reynolds?"

Her sister certainly knew how to cut right to the heart of things. "Not worried, exactly. But it would be unrealistic to think it's going to be easy or simple. It won't be either one. But it will be worth it, and I know I can trust him with my heart."

Summer reminded her sister that they better start their gift wrapping, and deftly changed the subject to past Christmases and favorite gifts. It also helped take her mind off worrying about Brody and the weather.

In spite of the snowfall, Brody arrived safe and sound. Evan had secured a house for Brody to rent for a week since it was impossible for him to rent anything in his own name.

He invited Summer and her family over for a special Christmas Eve dinner, and everyone assumed it would be catered. However, they were all surprised when they walked in to the wonderful aroma of Italian food simmering on the stove.

"The house is lovely," Leslie remarked. "How nicely the owners decorated it! I wonder why they went to all that trouble when they were going to rent it out over the holidays."

"According to Evan, they went rushing off to Philadelphia for the birth of their first grandchild, who decided to make his or her appearance a month early. I was all set to rent a smaller place when this one became available. I don't really need four bedrooms and two and a half baths, but I was pleased by the size of the living room and the dining room. And I liked the privacy of this location, where it's highly unlikely anyone would spot me.

"The other advantage," Brody continued, "is that I want all of you to feel free to spend as much time here as you would like before Summer and I leave for New York City." He looked around for Autumn's fiancé, commenting that he was surprised he had not joined them.

Autumn quickly explained, "His brother is in the military, and they literally just found out on the twenty-second that he was going to be able to come for the holidays." No one expressed their curiosity about why she had not chosen to go with him.

Brody then took them on a tour of the main living floor of the house, ending in the kitchen. Pots and pans covered the gray granite countertops. He shrugged as everyone's eyes widened at the sight. "I have a tendency to use every pot and pan when I'm cooking. Hence the reason my house has a restaurant-sized dishwasher."

Autumn lifted the lid of a large pot of garlic-laced spaghetti sauce. "It smells heavenly." She took one of the few remaining clean spoons on the counter and took a small taste. "Tastes heavenly, too."

"You can thank my grandmother Lucia. It was her recipe." His eyes shone with unshed tears, and his voice was thick with emotion. "She was so dear to my heart. We lost her when I was still a teenager."

Shawn broke the somber mood and rubbed his stomach. "When do we eat?" His appetite was legendary. "And more importantly, what are you serving?"

"I didn't have time to make homemade pasta, but—" He stopped when Summer rolled her eyes. "What? You don't believe me? Grandma Lucia would be *horrified* to think I was serving you store-bought pasta! I learned how to make it when I was eleven or twelve."

"I can't quite picture you going grocery shopping," Scott said. "Well, I mean without being mobbed. I can hear it now—'Martin Brody, aisle five!'"

They all laughed, Brody especially. "Well, you'd be right about that. When I'm at home, I get everything delivered. But fortunately, Evan has two assistants that do every conceivable errand for his clients, including shopping. All I had to do was e-mail Mandy a list and she took care of the rest."

Autumn peeked into the oven. "Did you make everything from scratch?"

"Yes. I'll have you know I slaved over that stove all day! We have yeast rolls and garlic bread, spaghetti a la Lucia, fettucine Alfredo with chicken, roasted vegetables, and several kinds of salads."

Autumn sighed loudly. "Summer, if you don't marry him, I might have to. I mean, really, the man can cook and sing? Dallas can't do either one."

Brody winked at her and smiled. "Then you'll just have to settle for me cooking Christmas Eve dinner every year."

Autumn stole a black olive from a tray by the sink. "I think I can live with that." There were times like this when Summer got the distinct impression that her and Dallas's wedding was never going to take place, but she had never broached that particular subject with her sister. She knew if Autumn did have any reservations, she would have to be the one to bring them up.

Since dinner was not due to be done for another hour, they all moved into the spacious living room to chat. Brody had turned the buffet table in the adjacent dining room into a bar with various beverages available.

"My favorite wine!" Leslie exclaimed happily.

"And my favorite beer," Scott said. "Well done—it's not easy to find."

"Summer was kind enough to give me some suggestions about what everyone likes to drink. We also have sparkling lemon water, hot spiced cider, and soft drinks."

Once they were all seated, beverages in hand, Summer eyed the tree and all the gifts underneath it. "Did the Rileys leave in such a hurry that they forgot to take their gifts?" The pile was truly impressive.

"No," Brody answered simply.

"Brody—you didn't," she scolded him. "We talked about this."

"Yes, we did, and then I ignored everything you said."

"But ... there are only nine of us here."

"I didn't want to leave out Adam and Natalie and Bethany. I'm sorry Natalie wasn't feeling well enough to join us, but I understand she is expecting again."

"We're beginning to wonder if she is expecting twins, but it's too soon to tell," Leslie said.

"The rest of you better get busy!" Scott advised. "Soon, they'll be either two or three up on the rest of you."

"Scott," Leslie said impatiently. "I think we'd like to see them get married first."

Brody later wondered if Scott and Leslie had purposely provided the perfect opening. "On that note ..." Brody began. All eyes turned to Summer, who suddenly could not breathe. "It gives me great pleasure to announce to all of you that Leslie and Scott have given me both their blessing and their approval." He pulled a familiar ring box out of his pocket and got down on one knee. "My Summer love, my world changed the first time I looked in your eyes. I knew my life would never be the same, and I also knew that if you didn't return my feelings, I would spend the rest of my life trying to win your heart. I want to give you my name. I want to spend every day for the rest of my life with you. And, more than anything, I want you to be the mother of my children. Will you do me the great honor of becoming my wife?"

Summer was speechless, so overcome with emotion that words failed her. It didn't matter that he had proposed once before, every bit as beautifully the second time as the first. It didn't matter that he had placed the ring on her finger before, and that had already married her. This was even more special. He had taken the time to ask her parents for her hand in marriage—he was laying his emotions bare in front of her family. When she glanced at her mother and her sister, they had tears streaming down their cheeks as well.

"I'm waiting for your answer," he reminded her gently.

"Yes, yes! Of course!" Now that she had found her voice, she could hardly stop talking. "Was there any doubt about what my answer would be? I've loved you since the first time I saw you, and I can't picture my life without you."

Brody circled her waist with his arms and twirled her around in a circle until she was dizzy before kissing her passionately. When her father coughed discreetly, they broke apart. Brody placed the ring on her finger, knowing, of course, that it would be a perfect fit, much the same way they for each other. The flawless sparkling two-carat emerald ring still could not match the light in her eyes.

Summer was immediately surrounded by the women in her life hugging her, kissing her, and admiring the ring.

As Scott looked at Brody and then his daughter, it was difficult to tell which one of them was more excited. He had always wondered what kind of man would steal the heart of his firstborn daughter, but he certainly never expected it to be this man. The man they had all seen accepting awards on television, whose face had graced the cover of numerous magazines, whose music had filled the house and who had written a beautiful love song for his daughter. Even though he loved both his girls equally, he and Summer were much more alike in temperament and personality, and he was a little closer to her than he was to Autumn.

When he reached out to hug his daughter, Leslie's phone rang and she stepped away briefly. In all the commotion, no one else had heard it ring. "Yes, Lynn," she said to Brody's mother. "We are all here celebrating an engagement. I have to say, your son really has a way with words. His proposal was very touching. I wish you were here to celebrate with us, but I understand you and Mitch had travel plans you couldn't change."

"Brody thinks we're in Aspen at his ski chalet. We usually go there for a week at Christmastime, but when he told us he was planning to propose, we rescheduled our flights. We're actually here, on the side porch! Can you let us in so we can surprise him?"

No one noticed her slip away. Moments later, Lynn and Mitch followed her into the house.

"We heard there was a celebration going on here, and we didn't want to miss it!" Lynn said as she approached her son, wrapping him in a tight hug.

"Mom! Dad!" His surprise and pleasure were evident in his smile. "I thought you were in Aspen with Bailey and Brennan and the Thompsons."

"We're not leaving until the twenty-seventh. Since Bailey and Brennan had invited friends to join them, they couldn't change their flights, but I'm sure they are thrilled for both of you."

Mitch shook his son's hand and then turned to Summer. "Lynn and I couldn't be happier. We brought some champagne to toast the happy occasion. Brody, let's go in the kitchen and uncork it!"

Lynn turned to her future daughter-in-law and could not hold back her tears of joy. "I will never forget the morning after you met. Brody called to tell me he had met the woman he was going to marry, and even though miles separated us, I could hear the love in his voice and the conviction in his heart. I prayed that his feelings would be reciprocated. I know what a force of nature my son can be, and I could only hope he was not headed for heartbreak."

Summer took Lynn's hands in hers and spoke from her heart. "Nothing could have prepared me for what I felt when his eyes met mine and he reached out to take both of my hands in his. There is no other way to describe it except to say it was love at first sight, but I never dreamed he would feel the same way about me. I feel like I'm living in a fairy tale, and every morning I expect to wake up to discover that it has all been a lovely dream."

Mitch and Brody returned with two bottles of champagne and one of sparkling wine. As soon as everyone had a glass, Mitch spoke first. "Summer, welcome to the family! Lynn and I know our son's heart will be safe with you."

Scott cleared his voice to speak when Leslie put a hand on his arm. "Lynn, Mitch, Brody—I have to say that this whole thing has taken us all by surprise, me most of all. But when Brody showed up to ask for Summer's hand in marriage, we knew his feelings for her were real."

"We were touched by his gesture," Scott said. "Our girl has always been old-fashioned, and the fact that Brody not only knew and accepted that, but also respected it, went a long way toward us accepting him into the family. So, let's all raise a glass to the happy couple!"

After a joyful toast, Lynn and Leslie helped finish up in the kitchen so Brody and Summer could enjoy their moment. Naturally, the conversation turned to wedding plans: where, when, small, large, public, private? Both Summer and Brody had a hard time acting as though they hadn't already talked about some of the details.

Brody took Summer's hand and looked at her fondly. "Well, I think I know Summer well enough to know that she will want something private and small, as do I. Evan will have to work overtime to make sure that no details are made public. And, to his credit, he has handled the weddings of some of his biggest clients over the years, so I'm sure he will have a lot of suggestions."

When everyone moved into the dining room, the wedding discussion continued. Summer was quick to point out that they did not want their wedding to upstage that of Autumn and Dallas. She turned to Brody as though this were the first time the subject had come up and asked, "What do you think about a fall wedding?"

He kissed her hand and answered that he wanted her to have the wedding of her dreams, and that the time and place and date were all hers to decide. His father laughed. "Lynn and I sure raised a smart son!"

"Happy wife, happy life," Scott added, and everyone nodded in agreement.

Chapter Twelve

ॐ

After dinner, there was a round of phone calls to family members that were not present. Summer and Brody had first advised everyone that they thought it best to not make the engagement public quite yet.

Brody then announced to Summer and her family that it was the Martin family tradition to open one gift each on Christmas Eve. As they all moved back to the living room, Summer took in the impressive pile of gifts and remarked again that he had gone overboard.

"Get used to it, my future wife," he said with both humor and sincerity. "There is nothing wrong with spoiling the people you love. And since we will soon all be family, this year is not about just spoiling you—it's also about spoiling the people you love."

Before the first present was opened, there was a knock on the door before Evan entered. He declined the opportunity to join them since he had to get home to his own family, but he congratulated the newly engaged couple and handed Brody a set of keys. "It wasn't easy, but they finally agreed to your terms. You're a hard man to say no to!"

Everyone, including Summer, was mystified by this latest turn of events, but Brody simply led them all outside. There in the driveway was a 1963 Corvette convertible that looked very familiar. Summer obviously couldn't ask if this was the exact same car they had driven to their first wedding ceremony, but when she looked at Brody, he gave her a little nod and said, "Surprise!"

For the second time that night, Summer was speechless. This wasn't just a great car; it was the very car that had delivered her to the man of her dreams on the night of their first wedding. She walked around it in a fog, and then she noticed the vanity plate and read it out loud so softly, it was hard to hear her. "BSM 921."

"BSM 921?" Kyra asked. "What is the significance of that?"

"It's the day we met. My birthday, September twenty-first."

"And our initials," Brody added. "I hope that wasn't presumptuous of me. I guess I was assuming you would want to take my name."

She threw her arms around him. "I can't wait to take your name."

As they went back into the house, Summer was wishing she had something for him that was equally surprising and exciting. She had a few ideas simmering but there were still details to work out.

Even though all of Brody's presents for Summer and her family members were impressive and thoughtful, nothing could match the car and the significance of it known only to the two of them. She couldn't help but smile the whole time they opened their pre-Christmas gifts.

Leslie and Scott were particularly pleased, but also overwhelmed with the generous gift Brody presented to the two of them. Brody just shrugged. "A certain someone told me you were considering a Caribbean cruise for your upcoming wedding anniversary. This gift certificate will cover all the expenses for the seven-day cruise of your choice."

Leslie tried to protest to no avail. Lynn jumped in and said, "We already exchanged gifts, thinking we would not be together on Christmas Day. He gave us one, too. How fun would it be for the four of us to go together!"

Much like their gathering on Thanksgiving evening, the conversation flowed effortlessly. Summer couldn't help but think everyone got along like they had been family friends for years. At times, she wondered if it was all just too good to be true.

As the evening wore on, the weather started to deteriorate. Summer and her family soon left for home, and Brody's parents elected to stay with him.

Leslie and Scott were hosting a Christmas brunch the following day, and Lynn and Mitch were happy to accept her invitation to join them. "We have plenty of room," Leslie said, "and plenty of food!"

"I'll bring the rest of the gifts," Brody said. "I still have a few surprises up my sleeve."

Summer just sighed, knowing arguing would be useless, and laid her head on his shoulder. "You've already spoiled me for other men."

"And that was my plan. You're stuck with me now."

"Well, I'm quite sure there are thousands upon thousands of women who would gladly trade places with me if you ever get tired of me."

"Probably millions," Autumn couldn't help but add.

"Well, your sister is one in a million." Brody winked.

Autumn just rolled her eyes. "I'm going out to the car now so you two can get all gushy and romantic without an audience."

"I'll be right there, sis."

"Oh, just kiss the man already!" Autumn called out as she walked away.

Summer was happy to comply, grateful to have a moment alone so she could ask the question that had been on her mind all evening. "I can't believe you bought that car. I was right, wasn't I? It is the same car we drove to our first ceremony?"

"It is. It was owned by a classic car rental company. Apparently, Evan had a hard time getting them to agree to sell it, but price was literally no object."

"You do know you don't have to spoil me with material things, don't you? I love you for you, not because you're a superstar."

"And that is exactly why I love you. As soon as I became famous, I worried that it was going to be hard to judge when someone truly cared about me and not just what I could do for her, or give to her. I wanted someone to love me in spite of my fame, and not because of it. And I know in my heart that you do."

Summer was on cloud nine, and wondered if she would ever come down. The rest of the evening consisted of her parents and her sister offering up their opinions and suggestions about not just the where and when, but also about what life was going to be like once Summer and Brody were wed. Her mother, in particular, was concerned about the impact having a famous son-in-law would have on the entire family, but nothing could dim Summer's happiness.

The following morning, everyone at the Reynolds's' home was up bright and early, exchanging family gifts and preparing for the arrival of Brody and his family.

Something suddenly occurred to Scott. He asked where Summer was planning to store the Corvette, as she did not have a garage at her apartment. "You could keep it here," he suggested, and they all laughed. "I could take her out for a spin every once in a while. You know, when you're busy at work or helping Autumn plan her wedding."

"There's not going to be a wedding," Autumn announced matter-of-factly. For the first time, Summer noticed that her sister's ring finger was bare.

"What?!" Summer exclaimed, trying to act shocked even though she had seen this coming.

"What happened?" Leslie echoed.

"Blame it on Brody," Autumn said unhappily.

Now Summer was completely confused. "Brody? What are you talking about?"

"We've all seen the way he looks at you. Dallas has never once, in all our years together, ever looked at me that way. I just woke up this morning and thought to myself, 'I want what Summer has.'" At her sister's horrified expression, Autumn laughed. "I don't mean I want Brody. I want the kind of love you have found with Brody. So, I called Dallas and told him the engagement was off."

Summer, while not entirely surprised by this turn of events, was surprised that her sister wanted the whole fairy-tale romance that she was so quick to say was unrealistic. Autumn always approached everything, including her love life, very matter-of-factly. She was the one with her feet on the ground, while Summer was the one with her head in the clouds.

Summer twisted her engagement ring around and around on her finger, hurting for her sister while simultaneously feeling relief. She knew

Autumn had made the right decision if she wasn't one hundred percent sure marrying Dallas was the right decision.

Autumn could sense Summer's discomfort and reached out to hug her. "Don't let my news spoil your excitement. You found yourself a true treasure, and I could not be happier for you. The only thing on my mind is finding a new place to live." She looked at her parents. "I know I can stay here for the short term, but I really need to think about a place of my own."

Brody and his family soon arrived, and they agreed to table the discussion until later.

Mitch and Lynn arrived bearing a wine and cheese basket, and Brody had so many gifts, it took several trips to bring them all in. After brunch, they moved to the living room and Brody said, "I had a thought last night after everyone left. I was thinking about when we watched *Somewhere in Time* and you said you had always wanted to stay at the Grand Hotel on Mackinac Island. What would you think about that as a wedding location?"

They shared a secret smile, and she hugged him enthusiastically. "I love it! What a wonderful suggestion! Mom—" She went to call out to her, but Leslie was already behind her.

"I heard. That is a wonderful suggestion. I've seen the movie as well, and I can't think of a more romantic location."

Summer could not think of one single thing that would have made her any happier than she was right now. So, she was completely unprepared for Brody's final two special gifts for her.

He called everyone around and opened up his laptop. "This is a little hard to recognize for what it's going to be, but I also brought the drawings along."

The first photos were of the outside of his home, a construction project obviously underway. She knew it was not the recording studio, as that was a totally separate building on the property.

Before she could ask what they were looking at, he moved the screen to show interior photos. It looked like a large unfinished room with a lot of beautiful built-in wooden shelves. Recognition dawned on Autumn's face as she recalled a private conversation she had had with Brody right before Thanksgiving.

"You're building her a library," she breathed in a voice full of wonder.

Summer turned to Brody, her eyes full of questions. "You're building me a library?"

"I know we haven't talked about this, but once we're married, it will be impossible for you to work somewhere. I know you want to continue to work, but it just won't be practical, so I came up with what might be a solution." He nodded approvingly at Autumn. "Your sister is actually the one who gave me this suggestion."

Summer looked questioningly at Autumn, who said, "Remember what you said you wanted to be when you grew up?"

The pieces of the puzzle finally clicked into place. "I wanted to write children's books."

"And so, my love, I am building you a space where you can write, where you can read to our children when they come along. Who knows? Maybe someday you'll be more famous than I am." That brought a round of laughter, but he was completely serious. "And, to help you fulfill your childhood dream, this kind of goes along with the library theme." He handed her a small envelope that looked suspiciously like an invitation.

When Summer opened it, she gasped aloud. This was more surprising than the car, but not any less meaningful. She was struck totally speechless once again at his ability to give her exactly what she wanted.

"Are you going to tell us what it is?" Autumn inquired.

"It's an invitation to an online writing seminar with a children's book author!"

"Not just any children's book author," Brody prompted. Seeing the confusion on her face, he realized Summer had not make the connection to who the author was. "It's with Lily Winters, whose pen name is Lillian Frost."

"Lillian Frost? *The* Lillian Frost?"

"Is there more than one Lillian Frost?"

Summer threw herself into Brody's arms. "She only offers these writing seminars to a few select people every few years! How did you manage this?"

Brody just shrugged and said his usual line—"I know a guy …"— and everyone but Summer laughed. She was still wondering how he had managed to pull this off, because she suspected that this invitation had been even harder for him to arrange than the purchase of the car.

The final gifts of the day were identical boxes for Summer, Autumn, and their parents. As they all opened them, Summer looked at Brody, confusion and curiosity evident in her eyes. "You bought us all new phones?"

"These are special, one-of-a kind phones. My parents have them, and so do all my siblings.

They have new untraceable phone numbers. For now, you can all continue to use your regular phones, but once we decide to make news of our engagement public, all of your lives will change in ways you never imagined. You will all be inundated with calls from the press, radio stations, television producers. Hopefully that won't last long, but you need to be prepared."

Summer turned hers on to discover that there were already several numbers, none of which were Brody's, preprogrammed into the phone. "So, who are speed dial one, two, and three?"

"Evan is speed dial number one, and his assistants can be reached at numbers two and three. If you're ever in trouble and I'm out of town touring, you need to call one of them. They are also both skilled in self-defense, and if they can't get to you quickly, they will send someone who can."

"And why do you think I might need someone with that particular skill set?"

"The paparazzi can be brutal, in your face with cameras and endless questions. They'll follow you into a grocery store or a restroom stall. Then there are the people you haven't seen in years who might come out of the woodwork. And maybe even people like Paul."

"Paul? My ex-boyfriend Paul? Why on earth do you think I might hear from him?" When she looked at Brody, he had a surprisingly guilty look on his face. "What?" she demanded. "What do you know that I don't?"

Autumn cleared her throat. "I'm the one you should be angry with, not Brody. I told him Paul tried to call me a couple of times, wanting to know where you were living and where you were working. Honestly, it worried me a little—it all seemed a little stalker-like, and I was afraid of what he might do once he found out about the two of you. I never liked him to begin with, and once he showed his true colors, I wondered what else he might be hiding."

Summer thought they were a little too worried about Paul when that relationship had ended more than a couple of years ago, but she reassured them both that she would let Brody and Evan know immediately if Paul was ever successful in tracking her down.

Chapter Thirteen

B rody and Summer spent every day together until it was time to leave for New York. Blake and Cassidy were joining them, and Cassidy's parents had agreed to watch their young daughter so they could have some quality time together. However, they were flying commercial and would not be arriving until the thirtieth. Brody was hesitant to tell Summer in case she thought he had planned it that way in order to stage a seduction.

He had no way of knowing that she was planning one herself.

When they took off, Summer turned to Brody and said, "I hope I never start to take this for granted."

"Me?"

"No, everything that comes along with who and what you are. I've been on uncomfortably crowded flights, dealt with flight cancellations, lost luggage, you name it."

"I'm thinking about how nice it will be to travel this way with our children. How many do you want?"

"Oh, at least five." She was really only half kidding. "As long as one of them is an impish little boy with his famous father's heart-stopping smile and tiger eyes."

"Tiger eyes?" he questioned. She blushed in response.

"The first time I met you, I thought …" she trailed off, embarrassed to finish her comment.

"You can't leave me in suspense!" he admonished. "Now you've got me curious. I've heard of bedroom eyes, but not tiger eyes."

She sighed, deciding she might as well tell him about her initial impression of him. "When I looked in your eyes, all I could think about was a tiger and what it would be like to try to tame you."

Now it was Brody's turn to blush, which seldom happened. "Honey, I have all kinds of images in my head now. And if we were already married, I'd take you in the back where the bed is and—"

"May I remind you we're already married?" She was more than ready to head to the nearest bed.

"I meant in the eyes of your parents. And mine! The first time I make love to you, I don't want anything between us." She raised her eyebrow questioningly. "No condoms," he whispered. "Just skin on skin. I want you to feel every inch of me the first time we make love." Before he could describe in detail everything he planned to do to her and with her, the pilot interrupted him.

"Mr. Martin, Miss Reynolds, we're approaching Rockefeller Center. If you look down, you can catch a glimpse of the tree. It will stay lit for another ten days or so. I've read that an average of five hundred thousand people visit the tree each day."

Summer knew seeing the tree was one of the most popular things to do at Christmastime in New York City, but she'd had no idea the number was that high.

"I wish we could see the tree this year, but it's just not possible." Brody sounded depressed, once again wishing he was just a normal guy that no one would recognize on the street. "Sometimes I wonder if I made a mistake, pressuring you into the quickie Vegas wedding. Your life with me will never be normal."

Summer was astonished to think he might honestly believe she would ever want to be with anyone but him. "I don't want normal. I want you." Once the words were out of her mouth, she realized how they sounded, and they both laughed.

"As much as I want you, I'm not sure I'm being very fair to you. Selfishly, I want nothing more than to be the only man in your life, and in your bed."

"And I want to be the only woman in your life, and in your bed. Every night, I go to bed dreaming about taking you in my hand and my mouth and my body. You are going to be my first, my last, my only."

He later wondered what might have happened in that moment if they had not been on their final approach to the airport. He ached to make love to her, body, mind, and soul. He wanted to ravish her, consume her, make her quiver with anticipation and need as he slowly slid into her untouched body and pushed her over the edge of a passion she had never experienced before. He had never experienced such an all-consuming blaze of desire.

"I still wish I could show you the city the way you deserve to see it. But for now, I need you to realize that the price of my fame comes at a personal cost. It has never bothered me, but I fear the day will come when it will bother you."

She shook her head in disagreement. "That day will never come. I don't love you more because you're famous, and I don't love you any less because of it. You are who you are, and it is what it is."

As they approached the small private airstrip, Brody explained that he had made arrangements for them to have a car at their disposal. "I've used this car service before, and they are very discreet. Limos in the city are everywhere, so no one will think twice about who might be in it. I do plan to show you some of the sights. And you don't need to worry about the driver—Carl is the chauffeur I always request, and I'm sure he would be happy to step out of the car and take your picture wherever and whenever you might like."

She nodded, her expression serious.

"Someday," he told her, "when the country music world has turned their attention to the next big thing, I will take you to all the places we can't go now."

Summer smiled at the notion that there would ever come a day when the screaming female fans would move on and simply pass him by on the street. "For now, all I want is you. But I do have to admit, I want to scream from the rooftops that you chose me. You chose me to be your wife, to share your bed, to bear your children."

Brody laughed and brought her close. He thought it was ironic that Summer wanted to flaunt their relationship to the world because in so many ways, she was very reserved. She had a small circle of close friends, but otherwise, she was quite a private person.

She started twisting her engagement ring around on her finger. "Should I take this off? What if Carl notices it?" She went to put her gloves back on when Brody stopped her.

"It'll be fine," he reassured her, but she turned it around anyway so that the emerald was not visible.

When they got off the plane, the air was cold, crisp. Light snow-flakes drifted lazily to the ground. The pilot took their luggage to the limo and greeted their driver like an old friend.

"Looks like they know each other," she observed.

"They do. Jason is one of two pilots I use frequently, and Carl has been driving me for years. I have, in fact, requested him in other cities, too. The car service operates in all the major cities, and I have some-times had Carl flown in so he could drive me around."

As they walked over to Carl, Brody made the introductions.

"What a lovely young lady." Carl reached out to shake Summer's hand and gave her a warm smile. "I've been driving Brody since shortly after he had his first number one. Because of him, I have seen a lot more of the country that I otherwise would have." He patted Brody's shoulder affectionately. "It has been my great pleasure to work for Mr. Martin."

"Carl, you know I consider you family. Someday I am going to con-vince you to move to Nashville and become my full-time driver!" This topic had obviously come up before. "And I am hoping that time might come sooner rather than later. You see, my friend Summer is not just a lovely young lady that I have brought along on this trip. She is my future wife."

The excitement in Carl's eyes was obvious. "I am very pleased to hear that. Miss Summer, you could not have chosen a more worthy man to share your life with. If I told you half of what he has done for me, you would hardly believe it."

"So, you'll consider making the move to Nashville? I realize you'll have to run it by Stephanie."

"When the time is right, I will share your wonderful news with her and we'll discuss it then. Until then, my lips are sealed."

"You're a good man, Carl."

As they walked to the car, Carl turned to Brody. "I just remembered something. The last time you were in the city, I picked you up for a clandestine appointment at Tiffany's. I'm assuming that was to make a certain special purchase?"

"It was," Brody confided.

"And now you're here to celebrate, to ring in the New Year together. My congratulations!"

Summer had her own ideas about how they should ring in the New Year together, but she kept her thoughts to herself.

Carl whisked them off to where they would be staying for the next few days, and the doorman made sure they were escorted quickly into the private elevator before anyone could recognize Brody.

When they reached the top floor and she stepped into the massive living room she felt much like she had in Vegas—like she had stepped onto a movie set. Two walls of the room were floor-to-ceiling glass, and the city lights were a sight to behold. "I have never in my life seen a sight like this," she said breathlessly.

"Nor have I," Brody spoke softly, but when she turned around, he was staring at her. "You are the most beautiful thing I have ever seen."

Compliments typically made her uncomfortable. Out of reflex, she laughed a bit nervously. "You're crazy. You forget, I saw that Victoria's Secret model who was your date at that awards show. She was drop-dead gorgeous and had the kind of body men lust over and women would kill to have."

He pulled her in for a searing, sensual kiss that made every nerve ending in his body come alive. "You are beautiful. You have a beautiful soul and a giving heart and eyes that mesmerize me. When I go to bed alone at night, all I can think about is that beautiful mouth wrapped around me. I have to confess ... no woman's voice has ever aroused me the way yours does."

The proof of his arousal was burning her to the core. "I have my own confession to make," she said, voice husky with passion and barely restrained need. "I have never felt such an aching need for a man's hands on me, a man's mouth on me, a man sliding into me until I was so overcome with desire and passion that I couldn't hold anything back."

He was seconds away from swooping her up in his arms and carrying her into the nearest bedroom when he stepped slightly away from her to take a breath.

She looked up at him with eyes full of love and a hint of hesitation. "Is something wrong?"

"No, nothing, my love. Hearing you tell me those things makes me want you even more. But I'm worried I won't be able to keep the promise I made to you to wait until we're married in the eyes of our friends and family … and to make matters more difficult, my brother and his wife aren't arriving until tomorrow. I told your parents we wouldn't be alone, and now it turns out that we will be. I don't want to take advantage of the situation, or of you."

She could tell he was struggling with his resolve, but she also knew that he was the only one for her, the only man she ever intended to take into both her heart and her bed. Before she could come up with a way to get him to give in to his desires, his cell phone rang.

Brody looked at the screen and whispered a soft "Damn."

"Who is it? A problem?"

"It's Evan. It must be an emergency, or he wouldn't be calling." It was hard to admit to himself that the interruption had come at the exact moment when he had, once again, been seconds away from seducing his wife. "What's up? Everything all set for tomorrow?"

"Yes, but Lucy and I have a problem."

"Talk to me," Brody said. "The shoe is never on the other foot. You make sure my life and my career run smoothly—what can I do for you?"

Summer was wishing she could hear the other side of the conversation, but thankfully, Brody did not look concerned enough to make her think their arrival in the city might have been spotted, or that Evan was calling with more serious news.

"They won't be here until tomorrow," Brody continued, then stopped to listen. "Where are you right now? Text me the address, and I'll have Carl come pick you up." She could hear Evan trying to argue with him on the other end, but Brody would hear nothing of it. "No, I am not going to let you stay in a hotel tonight, assuming you could even find one. There are three bedrooms here, plus the master suite. There's more than enough room for you and Lucy."

When Evan and Lucy arrived a little while later, they brought a feast with them from Brody's favorite restaurant. There was prime rib and twice-baked potatoes that literally melted in Summer's mouth along with roasted asparagus and crème brûlée for dessert.

"I think I could get used to eating like this," Summer said, patting her stomach. "But I also think I would need a new wardrobe."

"From now on," Evan advised, "your life is going to be a combination of gourmet dinners and road food. Not all of which is bad, by the way."

"And my tour bus does have a kitchen," Brody advised. "Although I travel much more frequently by plane."

"Less chance of him being mobbed by fans," Evan chuckled. "There was this one time in Cincinnati—"

Brody cut him off before he could continue. "Please, not the Cincinnati story! Tell her about Portland or Cleveland or Buffalo."

Summer's eyes twinkled with delight and she turned to Evan. "Now I *have* to hear the Cincinnati story."

"There was a mother and daughter at the meet and greet. The mother was obviously dressed in a way that would suggest she was trying to pass herself off as Tina's sister, and not her mother. They were both dressed … how to say this tactfully …"

Brody snorted. "There is no way to say it tactfully. They looked like hookers."

Lucy had obviously heard this story before, but she laughed right along with Summer.

"Anyway," Evan continued, "it was supposedly Tina's birthday, and her mother had a special request. She asked if Brody would show them the tour bus. He normally would not have agreed, except for the fact that one of his bandmates and his wife and small child were using Brody's bus, and he was traveling on the other bus with the rest of the band members. So, the three of them were approaching the bus when the mother suddenly 'remembered' something and took off like a shot. The next thing Brody knows, Tina is trying to seduce him and telling him that no one needs to know about her. It could be their little secret."

"You left out the part about her telling me she wasn't wearing any underwear," Brody added with a groan, and Summer laughed so hard her sides hurt.

"We always figured their endgame was for Tina to show up two or three months later and claim Brody took advantage of her and got her pregnant. Needless to say, Tina and her mother were crossed off the list of people allowed to attend future meet and greets."

"Did she ever show up again, at a concert?"

"If she did, security kept her far, far away from me. But the truth is, most fans are respectful and just happy to get an autograph or a photo with me."

"That's all I was expecting," Summer acknowledged. "Then I walked backstage and it was indescribable." She paused for a moment, and then in the same breath both she and Brody said, "It was love at first sight."

Chapter Fourteen

๑

T he talk soon turned to other subjects, and the evening passed quickly. Brody was a notorious night owl, so when he suggested they should all turn in before eleven, Summer was taken by surprise.

"Join us in the morning?" Brody posed to both Evan and Lucy.

"Perhaps for the first half of the day. I have everything arranged, and Carl has your schedule."

It sounded to Summer like a business meeting when Brody turned toward her and said, "No questions. It's a surprise. All you need to know is that you need to be ready to go at seven a.m."

This was a surprise to her. "Seriously? Seven a.m.? I hope whatever you're planning will be worth it!"

Summer had a hard time sleeping that night, thinking about Brody right down the hall as she tried to doze off. So close, and yet so far. When she did finally fall asleep, she was confronted by vivid erotic dreams that left her feeling excited and nervous at the same time. She knew comparisons to other women would be inevitable. Even though part of her longed for Brody to make love to her, the other part was worried he would find her lacking, her inexperience a turnoff.

At 6:45, she was ready to go and advised Brody, somewhat irritably, that it would have been easier for her to get ready if she knew the plans for the day. All he did was laugh. "You know how much I like surprising you."

When Carl picked the four of them up, Summer still had no idea where they were going, as she was unfamiliar with the city. When Carl announced that they were almost at their first stop, Brody said, "Close your eyes, sweetheart. I'll let you know when you can open them."

She dutifully followed his instructions but was completely unprepared for the sight before her when she opened her eyes. Carl had pulled up in front of Serendipity 3, a location from one of her favorite movies.

"Oh my gosh!" she squealed with delight. "Are we going there? They don't look like they're open yet. What about crowds? Fans?"

Instead of answering her, Brody simply led her, Evan, and Lucy to the front door, which opened swiftly before they were ushered inside. Summer's gaze excitedly took in everything from the beautiful Tiffany-style lamps to the tins of frozen hot chocolate mix for sale.

The owner greeted Brody with a hug, and introductions were made. "We'll be working with a small crew this morning, all of whom have been with me for many years and know their jobs depend on their discretion. As we discussed in advance, you will have ninety minutes before we open to the public." He gestured to the staircase. "Brody, I believe you requested a special table."

When they went upstairs, Brody called her attention to a seating chart on the wall that pointed out where various celebrities had dined while there. He led her to one table where John Cusack and Kate Beckinsale had once shared a frozen hot chocolate, the signature drink of the restaurant.

"I know it's a bit early in the day, but I figured hot chocolate is basically a breakfast drink, so they'll be making one for us. The only question I have is this: What flavor do you want? Traditional chocolate? Mint? Chocolate peanut butter?"

"Traditional, please."

And so the first part of the morning went as such: frozen hot chocolate followed by breakfast, photos, and a signed cookbook for Summer to take home.

Before they departed, Summer looked at Brody in amazement. "Do you remember everything I've ever told you? I can't believe you remembered something as inconsequential as the fact that I collect cookbooks!"

"I do remember everything. And I also remember that you said you know how to ice skate, so our next stop is Wollman Rink."

She was thrilled and a bit nervous at the same time. "I hope I don't break a leg … it's been a few years. Do you skate?"

"I played hockey in high school and college, so it's been more than a few years for me."

"So, maybe just a drive by the rink? I don't want to hobble around on crutches the rest of the time we're here."

Evan added his two cents. "Brody, as both your agent and your friend, I think that's a good idea."

Carl dropped Evan and Lucy off at their hotel, and then Brody and Summer continued with their tour of the city. After a drive past the skating rink, their next stop was Central Park, where a beautiful horse-drawn carriage awaited them. "I thought this would be low-risk enough to take a chance. Evan knows our driver personally, and he has assured us he will keep us a safe distance from other carriages." Brody pulled on a pair of glasses, a knit cap, and a scarf. "This should fool anyone from a distance."

"Except maybe for Tina," Summer couldn't help but tease him.

Their ride through the park was both picturesque and romantic. The ground was coated with a light layer of snow, and Summer was enchanted. As they were snuggled up under a blanket, she remarked to Brody that he could not have planned a more perfect day.

The ride was nearing an end when their driver took them by Belvedere Castle, and Summer asked him to stop so she could hop out and take a few pictures. It had been her intention to take a picture of Brody in the carriage when he got out and joined her. "I gave Casey my phone. He's going to take a couple quick pictures, and then we'll get back in the carriage."

They struck a cute pose for a couple photos and Brody stole a kiss before they settled back in the carriage. They were so wrapped up in each other, they were unaware they had been spotted.

When they returned to the penthouse, Blake and Cassidy had arrived and were settling in.

"My future sister-in-law!" Blake said enthusiastically, wrapping

Summer in a hug. "I hope you're ready for life with this one. It'll be a crazy ride."

"But worth it, I'm sure," Summer replied as she hugged him and then Cassidy. "How long have you two been married?"

"Fortunately for me," Blake joked, "it was before Brody has his first number one. Otherwise, I might've worried she was marrying the brother of the next big thing, instead of an ordinary guy like me!"

This topic had obviously come up before. Cassidy shook her head. "Don't believe a word he says. I've been in love with him since the second grade … although he didn't notice me until I grew breasts and became a cheerleader."

"Sadly, she's serious," Blake acknowledged. "Teenage boys can be so shallow. Just ask my brother about his first crush, the girl before Katie." The brothers exchanged a look that indicated this was a story worth hearing.

"Must you?" Brody implored. "Last night, Evan brought up Cincinnati." That brought a round of laughter.

"Oh, trust me, this high school chick was like Tina in training."

Summer turned her luminous eyes toward Brody. "So, girls were propositioning you way back when you were in high school?"

"Okay, I'm not *quite* that old. And you have it backwards—I did everything in my power to try to get Angela to notice me. I was a sophomore, and she was a senior. My asking her to the prom was the subject of much ridicule. Interestingly enough, when I became famous, someone interviewed her and she said she had 'always regretted' turning down my invitation to prom."

"So, your first broken heart?"

"After that, he did the breaking," Blake said with a smirk. "Let's see if I can possibly remember them all." He started counting on his fingers. "After Katie there was Beth, Jody, Vanessa—should I go on?"

Summer said, "Please do," at the same time Brody said, "Please stop."

"He acted like he was quite the Romeo, but the truth is that most of those girls, he was just friends with. We weren't really worried about any of them until Elena came along. She always seemed just a little too ... calculating."

Cassidy interrupted, "How about we leave the subject of Brody's past romantic exploits alone and talk about how thrilled we are that he chose someone as sweet and special as Summer? We are all excited you will be part of our family."

"And I'm sure you're equally thrilled to welcome the new addition to your family in the spring! Do you know what you're having yet, or is it too soon?"

Blake's smile was as big and bright as the Empire State Building glowing in the distance. "You're the first to know. We're having a boy this time."

"How wonderful!" While Brody was thrilled for his brother, all he could think about was the day when Summer would be expecting their first son or daughter. He wanted to be there for every moment, from the first time they heard the baby's heartbeat until his son or daughter made their way into the world.

"Yes, it is, and I'm trying to convince Cassidy that being down in Times Square in the crowds tomorrow night might not be safe."

Cassidy, who was barely showing, dismissed it with a wave of her hand. "I refuse to let you wrap me in a bubble. We'll be fine. And once we have two children, our time to do wild and crazy things will be a lot more limited."

Now it was Summer's turn to think about doing wild and crazy things with Brody, mostly in the bedroom. She had packed some lingerie she had every intention of modeling for him, but since she was tired from their long day, she went to bed early and Brody stayed up with Blake and Cassidy.

The following morning, Blake was still trying to get Cassidy to change her mind with no success. They had a plan for what to do in case they became separated in the crowd, and they went down to Times Square hours before midnight.

Brody was concerned that Summer would have agreed to be part of the madness if he was not so recognizable, but she assured him their plan was preferable. They shared a romantic dinner for two and a bottle of wine. By 9:00 p.m., Summer was having a hard time keeping her eyes open. "I'm not sure how I'm going to make it to midnight."

"Do you want to take a short nap? I could wake you up around eleven."

"Do you want to take a short nap with me?" she asked playfully.

"You and I know perfectly well what will happen if we lie down next to each other. So, no."

"Then it's a no for me, too. I think I just had a bit too much wine. Once I'm in the fresh air, I'll be fine."

The rooftop garden area was a delight with comfy chaises and a storage bin that held blankets and battery-operated candles. Summer looked down at the throngs of people in Times Square and sighed. "I'm glad we're up here and not down there. It would be so easy to get pushed and shoved and separated. I hope Cassidy is all right."

Brody pulled Summer back so she was leaning against him and nibbled on her neck. "They'll be fine. Trust me, Blake won't let anything happen to her or the baby."

They made themselves comfortable, and Summer rested her head on Brody's shoulder. She closed her eyes and tried to picture their life together. She knew there would be ups and there would be downs. All she could really hope for was that he was honest with her, and that he put her and their children first. She didn't want him to walk away from the music business for her and resent her for it. She also didn't want to come to resent him for the sacrifices she would have to make in her life in order to create a new life with him.

She was feeling drowsy when Brody moved his hands under the blanket to caress her breasts. Even through the fabric of her sweater, he could feel her nipples pucker against him. "I can't wait to touch you," he whispered.

"Fireworks," she replied.

"Yes, there will most definitely be fireworks," he agreed, and then he heard some starting to go off in the distance. He had been so entranced by the feel of Summer, he hadn't realized that she was talking about a different kind of fireworks.

As much as they both enjoyed the sight of the fireworks and the Ball Drop, they had other things on their mind. Brody was trying hard to stick to his promise of not making love to her until their wedding night, and Summer was trying to let him know, wordlessly, that she was ready to take their relationship to the next level.

Chapter Fifteen

❧

Once the celebration was over, Summer was ready to turn in for the night. "I think I'll go take a bath and wind down. The bathroom in the master suite has a Jacuzzi big enough for two." She turned toward him and smiled seductively. "Care to join me?"

"You have no idea how tempting that sounds." He could picture her perfect breasts barely peeking out of the swirling water, his fingers trailing a path down her body. Instead of agreeing, he kissed her senseless. She could feel his desire pressing against her and thought she had finally won the battle.

"So … that's a yes?"

"You're such a temptress." He slid his tongue into her mouth with lazy, sensuous strokes as he imagined burying his head between her legs and pleasuring her until she exploded. He was on the edge of suggesting just that when he reminded himself that although they were alone for now, his brother and sister-in-law would be making their way upstairs soon. When he finally succumbed to his raging passion for her, he wanted to be able to make love to her in a hundred different ways all night long, with no one there to hear her screams when she came apart in his arms. "As much as I want to say yes, tonight is not the night."

Summer could tell he was on the verge of changing his mind, but she too was concerned about having an audience. And, if she was perfectly honest with herself, she was also afraid of disappointing him.

The bath and scented candles did not relax her as much as she had hoped, so before she turned in, she went to the kitchen to have another glass of wine. When she encountered Brody, she was taken by surprise. He was wearing a soft fluffy robe, his hair still wet from his shower. Her mind immediately went to picturing him in the shower, the water running off his long, lean body, and it was impossible to hold back her sigh.

"Is that what you're wearing to bed?" he managed to ask.

"I wasn't planning to wear it for long," she replied with a seductive smile. "But that, of course, was assuming that I would not be sleeping alone tonight." The lingerie she wore left little to the imagination, and he felt quite sure she had never worn anything so blatantly sexy before.

"Do you like it?" She moved closer to him and reached her hand inside his robe to stroke his hard, throbbing shaft. "I bought it in every color—fire-engine red, black, and a dusty-pink rose, the same color as my nipples." They were pressing up against the see-through fabric, begging to be touched. "I saved myself for you, but I'm tired of waiting."

"It's been hard for me, too," he replied, and he heard her throaty laugh in response.

"I can see that," she teased.

"I meant the waiting has been hard."

"It's not going to get any easier," she said matter-of-factly.

"That's true. And maybe it will be impossible for us to wait for our official wedding night, but there are a lot of reasons I'm not going to make love to you tonight. The first time I make love to you, I don't want to feel anything between us but skin. The first time I make love to you, I want it to be when we are ready to make babies. I want to feel your body clench around me. I want to come inside you, over and over and over again. I want to make you scream with passion and pleasure."

"If I promise not to scream, will you take me to your bed and make love to me? I bought condoms. I wasn't sure how many we might need, so I bought a dozen."

He took a small step back from her. If she kept touching him, he was going to explode. "I might be the one to scream," he admitted. "I know our first time will be your first time, but there is something else you need to realize. Even though the first time I make love to you will be special and wonderful, it will mean a lot more to both of us if we wait until we've said our vows in front of our friends and our family before taking that step."

"I know you're right," she admitted, feeling disappointed and sexually frustrated, but somehow loving him even more all at the same time.

"The gift of your virginity is something I will never take for granted. I know you don't understand, but I want to wait for our official wedding night to possess you totally and completely."

"Can I sleep next to you tonight if I promise not to try to seduce you?"

"Do you have a long flannel nightgown you can put on? Because otherwise, there is no way I'm going to be able to keep my hands off you."

In the end, she put on his college sweatshirt—even though it was so big, she was practically swimming in it—and a pair of yoga pants. She made him put on a pair of sweatpants and a long-sleeved T-shirt, and they both burst out laughing when they got into bed.

"This was not the bedroom scene I was expecting," she said. "But if you feel temped in the middle of the night to wake me up and have your way with me, you won't get any resistance from me."

Summer cuddled up close to Brody and put her head on his chest. "I can't wait until we can spend every night for the rest of our lives together."

It was a long night for both of them. It seemed like hours after he heard her soft, even breathing that he was finally able to drift off himself.

When morning arrived, they took separate showers despite her comment that they could save time and water if they took one together. They were enjoying some orange juice and buttery croissants when Blake and Cassidy finally appeared.

"So," Summer inquired, "how was it being down in that mob?"

Cassidy sat down to join them with a sigh and slathered raspberry jam on a croissant before answering. "It was fun," she replied as they all watched Blake shaking his head in disagreement.

"Not the word I would use," he said. "You guys had the right idea."

"The view from the rooftop garden was spectacular," Summer acknowledged, all the while thinking about Brody's wandering hands under the blanket.

Brody's thoughts mirrored hers. "Yes, it was," he somehow managed to say with a straight face.

When Summer started to blush, Cassidy changed the subject. "What's on the schedule for you two for today?"

"We're planning to do more sightseeing. I arranged for Carl to pick us up at two o'clock. You're welcome to join us if you'd like. We're planning to go—" He was interrupted when his phone rang with Evan's ringtone. "Happy New Year!" he said with a smile that almost instantly faded. "What? How did that happen?" He got up from the table, visibly upset, and moved into the other room to finish the call.

When he returned, they all looked at him with concern. Summer was suddenly overcome with a feeling of dread. "What did Evan want?"

"It seems we were spotted in Central Park, although from the grainy photo, it's not obvious it was us. But I'm afraid now that the chances of someone seeing us has increased dramatically."

"Do they know who I am?" As much as Summer wanted the world to know they were engaged, she did not want the cat out of the bag until they were ready to make a press announcement. They wanted to control the time and place.

"No, and at this point I'm not sure how they would find out your identity. We just need to be more vigilant. It might be best if Carl picks us up at separate locations."

He placed the call to Carl and they discussed the fact that Carl had been photographed with Brody previously, so arrangements were made to use a different driver that Carl trusted implicitly.

Blake suggested they get on the Internet to see what had actually been shared online, and they all gathered around his laptop. There was a distant shot of them kissing by the castle, but how anyone had made the leap to thinking it was Brody was a mystery to all of them.

Summer was ready to shrug the whole thing off when she started reading the comments. She thought she had known what to expect, but oh, how wrong she had been. She read one post after another, wondering what possessed people to make such assumptions about someone they didn't know a thing about. "Who is Martin's mystery girl? "Does she know how many have come before her?" "Does she know how many he has made come in his bed?" *Hmm ... I wouldn't mind knowing the answer to that one.*

"What total bullshit!" burst from Summer so vehemently, it took them all by surprise.

Brody had hoped they wouldn't face a trial by fire so soon after their secret engagement, but the other part of him recognized that she needed to accept the inevitable price of his fame sooner rather than later.

Fortunately, with no real proof, the speculation that Brody and a mystery woman were currently in the city faded. But for Summer, it was a glaring reminder of what she would be facing from here on out. They were not spotted again, but despite Brody's best attempts to cheer her up, he was not entirely successful.

When she arrived back home, her parents stopped by to hear about their trip. They were expecting a glowing report but disheartened to hear about the photo and, more importantly, her reaction to it. When they started fussing over her like she was a child, she came close to losing her composure.

"My identity is still a secret," she reminded them. "No one knows who I am, and no one knows Brody is engaged."

Her father tried to tread carefully. "But it was still a wake-up call, wasn't it?"

Summer waited for her mother to start talking about how this was just the tip of the iceberg, but she was surprised when she held back. "How are you going to handle getting together in the future?" was all her mother asked.

"I wish I knew," Summer admitted. "He's working on a new album and trying to decide what the first single should be. He's involved in the merchandising decisions, and soon he has to finalize who his opening acts are going to be for his summer tour. He's just as busy off the road as he is when he's touring. The only difference is, he's sleeping in his own bed each night."

"What does all that mean, honey?"

"We may not see each other again until mid-February. We want to spend his birthday and Valentine's Day together. So, I'll probably go to Nashville. Maybe his family will come, too, since they're every bit as close as we are. Which reminds me, have you made any plans for the cruise?"

Her mother nodded. "We're thinking about taking the cruise with Lynn and Mitch next January."

"I think the four of you will have a great time together. I'd love to go on a cruise someday, but it seems so impractical for us."

"Honey, I know you two love each other—anyone with eyes can see that. But is it worth everything you'll have to give up?" When she hesitated, the worry in her father's expression deepened.

"Dad, I am nowhere near ready to give up on him. I know we will never have what some people would consider a 'normal' life. We just have to figure out *our* normal."

Her mother was still fretting. "I'm afraid the news of your engagement will be discovered before you're ready to go public."

"And I have to wonder if the frenzy would die down if he announced he was off the market, or if that would just make people more curious to know who he was engaged to," her father said.

"Everyone would want to know the who-what-where-when details ... and we haven't gotten that far in the planning yet."

Chapter Sixteen

It was a long six weeks until she was able to see Brody again. One of the only things that had cheered her up was her sister moving into her apartment complex. Autumn had barely unpacked before she invited Summer over for a wine and cheese party with some of her new neighbors. Autumn had always been the more social twin, and she wasted no time in getting to know people. But when Summer was asked about whether there was anyone special in her life, she was hesitant and uncomfortable. She hated feeling like she was hiding something, and she had never been comfortable with half-truths.

In February, Brody sent his plane to pick Summer up and deliver her to Nashville for a combination birthday and Valentine's Day celebration. She decided to pack the fire-engine red lingerie, hoping that this time she might have a chance to wear it.

Evan was waiting for her at the airport. He explained that Brody was putting the finishing touches on a surprise for her and would be waiting at the house when they arrived.

Summer was not sure what she was expecting, but it was certainly not to discover there was a world-famous fashion designer there with a collection of bridal gowns for her to try on. Her mother was there, along with his mother and Autumn.

"How did you manage to keep this a secret?!"

"I knew you were wanting to find the perfect gown, and even though our engagement is not public yet, once that day does come, going shopping for a gown would be a logistical nightmare. So, instead of you going to the dresses, the dresses have come to you! And I knew, of course, that you would want your mother and Autumn there."

"And I invited myself," Lynn said. "Leslie assured me you wouldn't mind."

"Of course I don't mind." Summer hugged her future mother-in-law.

"I'm out of here!" Brody said. "You don't need me hanging around."

"It's bad luck," all the women said at once.

"When you're done, come fetch me." When he turned to leave the room, something suddenly occurred to him. "Antonio has assured me that there will be no charge for whatever gown you choose. His only condition was that when we choose to have a few wedding photos published, we mention you were wearing one of his designs. The press from that will be worth far more than the price of one of the gowns."

Summer and Autumn exchanged a look of both wonder and concern. Suddenly, this seemed very real. Summer had never dreamed that her wedding photos would one day be published in something like *People* magazine.

Antonio had indeed brought a number of different gowns in varying shades of white and ivory, most somewhat traditional. Brody knew his bride to be well enough to know she wouldn't want to wear something that was revealing in any way, even though he loved her curves.

Gown after gown was tried on and set aside. Summer felt the mermaid style was unflattering and potentially uncomfortable; she loved the strapless style but was a little too conscious of the way it accentuated her bustline. The only thing she was able to decide was that she did not want a stark white gown. Everyone agreed that an ivory shade was much more becoming.

By the end of it, Summer was disappointed she hadn't found the perfect gown, but Antonio was sweetly reassuring. "My dear Summer, I've had ladies try on hundreds of gowns before they find the perfect one. Now that I have a better idea what your preferences are, we can arrange another fitting whenever it suits you. I'm also leaving you with one of my design books. If you see a design you like, we can custom create your very own one-of-a-kind gown. Your gown will truly be a masterpiece that will never be recreated!"

Once he left, Summer drained the last of the champagne in her glass.

"What am I going to tell Brody? He'll be so disappointed. I don't want him to take it as a sign that I'm undecided about whether I want to marry him."

After some back and forth, Autumn managed to convince Summer that Brody knew full well nothing was going to change her mind about marrying him.

"Are you guys going to stay over? I'm sure you could use the guest house," Summer said, although she really wanted nothing more than to have Brody to herself.

"Autumn and I are going home on his plane," Leslie said with a smile.

"Sounds like you're starting to get used to all the perks that come along with having a famous future son-in-law," Summer couldn't help but tease her mother.

"I will admit, it beats flying commercial."

After they all said their goodbyes, Lynn left too. Summer was not left alone with her thoughts for long when Brody returned.

"How did it go? Not that I need any details about your selection," he was quick to add.

Summer burst into tears. "I didn't find one. They were all lovely and special, but none of them screamed 'Wear me when you walk down the aisle to marry your lifetime love.'"

"Your lifetime love …" he echoed. "Wait right here. Don't move—I'll be right back."

His idea of being "right back" stretched into more than thirty minutes. Summer was just getting ready to go find him when he returned.

"Sorry," he said, kissing the top of her head. "I suddenly remembered something I needed to take care of." She gave him a questioning look, but he didn't explain further.

"So, what's on the schedule for your birthday? Will your family be joining us to celebrate?"

"I don't want to celebrate with anyone but you," he confessed. "I can't believe I haven't seen you for forty-three days. It's the longest we've been apart. All I can think about is taking you in my arms and never letting you go. I want to sleep next to you and wake up next to you and—"

"Make love to me all night long?" she said hopefully. "As I recall, you said you wanted to feel my body clench around you. You want to slide slowly into my untouched body and come inside me, over and over and over again. You want to make me scream with passion and pleasure."

"All that is true. But you left out one of other important things I said: I want nothing but skin between us the first time we make love. I don't want to just make love to you—I want to make babies with you." When he kissed her with forty-three days of pent-up desire, his body reacted.

"And I want to show you your birthday present," she teased him before she deviously slipped her tongue into his mouth, tracing the corners of it as she imagined what it would be like to taste all of him. "I need ten minutes, then meet me upstairs, Brody." Summer decided it was time she took matters into her own hands. She knew if she took him in her hands—and in her mouth—he would not be able to hold back.

Six minutes was the longest he could wait. When he opened the door to the master bedroom, Summer was wearing her engagement ring, the fire-engine red lingerie, and the sexiest pair of high heels he had ever seen. She had long shapely legs, but the *V* at the juncture of her thighs interested him more than anything else. Before he could say a thing, she said, "I want to consummate our marriage."

"We could do … *other* things," he suggested, quickly losing his resolve to wait.

"I want to consummate our marriage," she repeated.

He was getting nearly as frustrated as she was. "And do you want to go to your parents two or three months from now and tell them you're pregnant? Or give birth to our first child only five months after our official wedding? Have you thought about how hurt our families would be if they knew we had married in secret and kept it from everyone?"

Her face fell. Moving slowly, she stepped out of the teddy. She *had* thought about all those things, and many others as well. And then, for the first time, she finally expressed the worry she had held in the deepest recesses of her heart.

"All evidence to the contrary, you obviously don't want to make love to me. So, what's behind that? Are you hoping at the end of the year, I'll ask for an annulment? Is this just some publicity stunt? Do you want the news of our engagement to mysteriously leak? Do you know who took our photo in New York?" Once she started talking, it seemed she was unable to stop. "Am I just a novelty to you? Your first virgin?" She could hardly believe she had been ready, willing, and able to offer herself up to him, and he was turning her advances down. *Again.* Whatever confidence she had felt about her ability to change his mind had suddenly evaporated, leaving her feeling as deflated as an old balloon.

Brody felt he knew her better than she knew herself; he was convinced she would be filled with regret if they did not wait. Before he could frame his thoughts in a way she could understand, she strode across the room and began pulling things out of her suitcase.

"I can't do this anymore," she announced in a trembling voice. "I think I should go home."

He didn't think she was serious until she started to take off her engagement ring.

"No, no, no!" he cried out in distress, rushing over to her. "You're wrong. You're wrong about all of it." He turned her tear-streaked face toward him. "I love you. I *want* you. I need you in a way I have never needed anyone before."

She refused to be swayed by all the pretty words. "Then you have a choice to make."

"If it's lose you or make love to you, then the choice is obvious."

"That's not what I meant. I know we had planned to wait longer to announce our engagement, to give us more time to get to know each other on a deeper level. Give our families more time to accept this."

"So, what are you saying?"

She pulled a T-shirt on without bothering with a bra. He was discouraged she was still getting dressed, but encouraged to see she had not taken the ring off.

"You need to either let me go, or you need to announce to the world that you're engaged. You don't need to give them my name and, in fact, I wish you wouldn't. It would be nice to keep that a secret for a while longer."

The relief on his face was obvious. "So, you still want to marry me? Well, stay married to me." He started to ramble. "I don't want to lose you. You mean more to me than anything else in my life ever has or ever will."

She started crying again, and he was at a loss as to how to both comfort her and convince her he was serious.

"What can I do?" he pleaded earnestly. He didn't want to make love to her right now to prove his love, but he was willing to do so if that was what she needed to feel reassured about their future.

"Can we just start this day over again?"

"You need to relax. Do you want to go take a bubble bath, or use the Jacuzzi?"

"A bubble bath," she nodded. "And a glass of wine."

He went into the master bath, dimmed the lights, and lit a candle. Somewhere in the bathroom he found a jar of scented bath beads left behind by one of his sisters.

When she walked into the bathroom, she was wearing his robe, but not her engagement ring. His heart stopped. "Why did you take it off?" he asked quietly.

"Oh, it's not what you think. I'm afraid it'll slip off if it gets wet. I always take it off before I take a shower."

He slipped the robe from her shoulders and kissed the side of her neck. "Red or white?"

Her thoughts were fuzzy. "What?"

"Wine. Red or white?"

She slipped into the lavender-scented water and sighed. "I loved to take bubble baths when I was little. I haven't taken one in years … but let's hold off on the wine until dinner."

When she joined him in the kitchen, she discovered he had ordered food from one of his favorite restaurants.

"You just missed Mandy," he said as he began to unpack bags of food that smelled absolutely heavenly. "I had her pick up a little bit of everything."

"The Loveless Café?" Summer inquired, reading the name on the bags. "I've never heard of it."

"Oh, trust me, once you have tasted their biscuits, you will never be the same. No one makes a biscuit like they do. I ordered enough to have some for breakfast in the morning along with their homemade preserves."

Once all the food was ready, Summer had a hard time deciding what to try first. Brody suggested a biscuit while they were still warm, and she moaned when she took her first bite. "These just melt in your mouth. Unless you ordered more than a dozen, there's no way we'll have any left for breakfast."

They dished up country ham, Nashville hot chicken, BBQ pulled pork, and side dishes of fried green tomatoes, grits, and slow-cooked green beans.

"Everything is delicious. I may never cook again."

"I hope you saved room for dessert. Their pecan pie is nothing short of spectacular."

In the end, they were both too full for pie, and they joked about having pie for breakfast because, sadly, there were no biscuits left.

After dinner Brody went to make a phone call, after which he showed Summer the progress that had been made on the library.

"In a couple of weeks, you should start to pick out furniture in case anything you want is on back order. I assumed you would prefer to pick out your writing desk and chair."

"I would," she nodded. "How are they coming on the recording studio? I hope you didn't put that aside so they could work on this."

He shook his head. "Two different crews. But if this looks a little different from the original drawings, it's because I decided to include a fireplace. I know it's a little impractical, but I thought you would like to have one in here."

"I would! You've thought of everything. I can't wait to see what surprises you have in store for me for Valentine's Day."

"I can think of only one thing that would make tomorrow perfect—announcing on Valentine's Day that I have found the love of my life."

"How do you plan to accomplish that on short notice? No, let me guess—you know a guy who knows a guy ..." That had become their private joke.

"Actually, you're not far off! I will be up bright and early tomorrow morning, and you will need to tune in to *Music City Morning* at eight o'clock. After that, the world will know who my heart belongs to."

Chapter Seventeen

W hen Summer woke up a little before seven, he was gone, presumably on his way to the television studio.

Shortly after 8:00, the show started and the host was interviewing a very distraught-looking Evan. Perhaps he had tried to talk Brody out of making this announcement? They were obviously waiting for Brody, who she assumed was running late.

At 8:30, after what seemed to be a lengthy commercial break, the host announced they had breaking news. *Finally!* Summer thought.

The host turned to Evan. "We have just received word that Martin Brody is not even in Nashville! He was seen in a little town in Georgia at six o'clock this morning accompanied by a woman. Evan, can you confirm that Martin and his lady love have eloped?"

Summer was momentarily shocked, and then started to scream at the television. "Eloped?!"

Before Evan had a chance to reply, they showed a photo that had come in from a local television station in Lancaster, Georgia, showing Brody standing next to a woman with someone who appeared to be a minister. It looked like he was giving them some sort of blessing. Their heads were bowed, and Brody's arm was around the woman's waist. It was hard to think it could be anything other than what it appeared to be. Did that make him a bigamist, or did that mean that their ceremony had been a sham?

She turned off the television and almost threw her cell phone across the room before she thought better of it and called her sister, who had already heard the news.

"I need to get out of here. Book me on the next plane or train or bus. I don't care if I have to change flights two or three times—just do it." She needed her normal phone until she heard back from Autumn with her flight information, but she took the special phone outside and threw it in the swimming pool. She considered doing the same thing with the ring, but she ended up leaving it alone on his bedside table. No note, no tearful letter of goodbye, although she did consider thanking him for not taking her virginity. She could still give that to her real husband someday.

In record time, Autumn had her booked on a flight and had arranged for a taxi to pick her up a couple of blocks away to take her to the airport.

"When I get to the airport, I need to ditch my cell phone. I'll buy a disposable one and call you with that number."

An hour later, she was at the airport about to board her flight, new TracFone in hand, when her cell rang with Brody's ringtone. She simply turned it off and dropped it into the nearest trash can. Her anger was starting to turn to sadness, but she kept remembering his refusal to make love to her. She had been prepared to give him the most precious gift she had, but he obviously didn't want it, or her. It destroyed her to admit to herself that she had fallen for a fantasy. The man behind the beautiful love songs was not the man the world, and Summer, thought he was. She had been naïve to think she was ever going to be enough for him.

The last leg of her journey was unexpectedly cancelled, so instead of waiting four hours for the next available flight, Summer decided to go the rest of the way home by bus.

She begged Autumn to come alone to pick her up. She was not ready to face her parents. She knew her mother would never say "I told you so," but she would be thinking it. They would all be thinking it. She was beyond relieved when she got off the bus and Autumn was the only one waiting for her.

Autumn was not prone to public displays of emotion, but when she saw her heartbroken sister, she started to cry.

"Dad wants to kill him. I told him to get in line behind me. Mom wants to call his mother and ask her how she feels about having a lying, cheating, two-timing bastard for a son. And don't get me started on what I'd like to say to Bailey and Brennan!"

They made their way slowly to Autumn's car arm in arm. "I always wondered, in the back of my mind, what he saw in me. Let's face it, we've seen pictures of the gorgeous women he has dated and bedded. So, what attracted him to an innocent twenty-two-year-old virgin?" She stopped short of telling Autumn she had thought they were already married. That would require an explanation she was not up to telling—not now, probably not ever.

"You could ask yourself that question from now until the end of time and you may never know. We all saw the initial spark when you two met; I don't think that was an act. And as much as I hate to ask you this …"

"Yes, I'm still a virgin, although I practically threw myself at the man—more than once—and he turned me down each time. I guess now I know why. I wasn't the only woman in his life. He needed to keep our relationship a secret so she wouldn't find out about me and I wouldn't find out about her."

"Any idea who she is?"

"Don't know. Don't care."

"We all destroyed the special phones so he can't reach any of us. Mom and Dad are getting us all new phones from a different carrier with unlisted numbers. Short of showing up at the house, or the library, he won't be able to track you down. Thank God you didn't marry him before he showed his true colors."

Summer was lost in her thoughts and stared out the window. At some point, she assumed, Evan would find a way to get in touch with her to untangle the Vegas wedding. Or … maybe not. How could he be legally wed to her and the mystery bride at the same time?

Summer arrived home to find her parents waiting in the driveway with a new vehicle she had never seen before already running. *A rental?* She didn't want to talk this to death, but she couldn't believe they were getting ready to go on a trip when she was at the lowest point in her life.

Her parents got out of the car and engulfed her in a hug. "You don't have to say anything," her mother said. "Just get in the car."

"Where are we going?"

"We're going to Aunt Sarah's lake cabin. They winterized it last year so they can stay there or rent it out all four seasons. It's a bit on the rustic side—no Wi-Fi, no cable. For the next four or five days, we will be cut off from the world."

Summer suddenly realized she had left her suitcase at Brody's house and had escaped with nothing more than her purse. "I need to pack."

Autumn slid into the back seat next to her. "No need, I packed for you. You don't need to worry about hearing or seeing any news about Brody. If you want to talk about what happened, you can; if you don't, we won't pressure you about it."

Summer leaned back and sighed, exhausted. "Sounds good to me." She closed her eyes and tried to sleep but images of Brody kept popping up, unwanted. Image after image plagued her. *The first time their eyes met. The first kiss they shared. Brody down on one knee at the Vegas chapel. Brody building the library for her. Brody writing the song for her.* It all seemed so real, and she started to have doubts.

The next images that crowded her vision were of her standing half naked before him, him making excuses as to why he would not make love to her. Was he thinking of the other woman when he was aroused? Had he ever had any true feelings for her? As much as she wanted answers, she knew in all likelihood she would never get them. Or at least not any she could believe.

Summer had always thought she was a good judge of character, Paul aside. She considered herself to be somewhat cautious, perhaps naïve, but this had both blindsided her and devastated her.

They ended up staying at the cabin for five days. There was fresh snow during their stay, and they went snowshoeing and cross-country skiing. In the evenings, they read by the fire and played board games. Every night it got a little easier to fall asleep, but the last night, all Summer could think about was what she would be facing when she returned to real life. Would there be pictures everywhere of Brody and his new wife? Whatever she was dreading and expecting, however, was nothing like what she actually faced when they returned home.

Their neighbors, Joyce and Mike Warren, came over when they saw them pull in to fill them in on what little they knew about what had transpired in their absence.

"Every day," Mrs. Warren confided, "a car pulled up in front of your house and a man named Evan came knocking on our door to see if we knew where you were. One day, a young woman came looking for you. Then yesterday, someone dropped this off." She handed Summer a package addressed to her in Brody's handwriting.

"I don't care what's in there." She handed it to her mother. "Burn it, destroy it, send it back to him. I don't care." And with that, she went upstairs to her room.

Shortly after, the Warrens left too. They were partway down the sidewalk when Mr. Warren turned back around. "We forgot to mention, a very heartbroken-looking young man also came by every day and stared at your front door. He looked familiar, but I don't know who he was. I won't be surprised if he shows up again tomorrow. You might want to call the police."

Summer's parents were mystified by this turn of events, but they warned Autumn to stay out of it. Autumn, however, was too anxious to find some kind of answers for her sister, whether she liked them or not. She knew Summer would need closure.

The first thing Autumn did when she went up to her room was get on the Internet. Without even having to type in Brody's name, there were headlines after headlines at the top of the news page. She clicked on a link that took her to a video from the airport where someone had retrieved Summer's cell phone—she had discarded it without thinking to remove the battery so it couldn't be tracked. Another one featured someone at the bus station asking questions. And then she found a clip from a press conference at which a heartfelt plea from someone named Katie Bauer asked Summer to reach out to her. Katie's name was familiar, but Autumn couldn't place it.

Autumn only hesitated for a moment before she opened the package Brody had left for Summer and popped the disc into her computer. Brody was sitting next to a woman who Autumn assumed was Katie. *Was Katie the one in the chapel in Georgia?* She almost turned it off, but something stopped her.

"Summer," the woman pleaded, tears in her eyes. "We know what you and the rest of the world thought when that picture of us surfaced. Brody's heart belongs to only you. If someone else is watching this video, you need to tell Summer to watch it. She knows who I am, although we have never met in person. But what she doesn't know is why Brody was standing next to me in the chapel." Autumn stopped the video and went to get Summer.

Summer was adamant that she did not care what, or who, was in the video, but Autumn was equally insistent that she needed to see it. Summer was about to shut her bedroom door in Autumn's face when Autumn asked, "Who is Katie? She wants you to call her."

That was all it took for Summer to fly past Autumn into her room. "Play it!" she demanded.

"Should I go get Mom and Dad?"

"No, just play it."

The video began again, and when Katie told her heart-wrenching story, Summer and Autumn were both sobbing.

"When Allison was born, the doctors told us she would not survive the night. Brody sent his plane to get the world's best neonatal surgeon and brought him to the hospital. Brody took me to the hospital chapel so we could pray for her while Brian stayed by Allison's bedside. It was touch and go, but they performed emergency surgery, and she survived. It will be a long road to recovery, but it looks like my daughter is a little fighter.

"Summer, I just know if Brody had not arrived with that surgeon, our daughter would not have made it. She is alive because of him. I don't know why he didn't wake you up to tell you what was going on; I think he thought he could get back to Nashville in time for his appearance on *Music City Morning,* where he had planned to announce your engagement."

Brody started to talk. "I couldn't reach Evan before *Music City Morning* started. When the show was over, I sent him to the house to tell you what was going on, but you were gone. I looked everywhere. Evan and I came to your house every day. I sent Evan to the library. I hired a private investigator to find you, but all he was able to find out was that your parents had purchased a new SUV. No one knew where you were, or if they did, they weren't about to tell us."

He took a deep breath before he continued. "I don't know how long you'll be cut off from the world, but I hope you or someone in your family sees my press conference at nine a.m. on the twentieth, and I hope that answers whatever lingering questions or doubts you might have. I love you, and I hope with all my heart that you still love me."

Chapter Eighteen

❧

S ummer was relieved, rendered speechless by the flood of emotions. How could she have misjudged him so thoroughly? She questioned if she even deserved his love if she had been so quick to jump to conclusions without giving him a chance to explain.

She called her parents upstairs and watched the video again with them. They had a long talk about how Summer could handle herself going forward if she still wanted a future with Brody.

It took all the strength she had not to call him that night, but she knew the wise decision was to wait to watch his press conference in the morning and go from there.

The next morning when he stood at the podium, he looked like an exhausted, devastated man. "Summer, I hope you or someone you know is watching this. I am here today to announce my retirement from the music business. All the fans that bought tickets to my summer show will get refunds and free advanced copies of my final CD. I hope with all my heart that the gossip and wild speculation has not cost me the heart of the woman I love. She means more to me than fame and success and awards, and all I want is to marry her and be the father to her children. That is all. I will not be taking any questions."

The press, of course, went crazy. "Who is Summer?" The questions kept coming even though he had stepped away from the microphone. "Who was with you in the chapel?" Brody refused to answer any questions, and Evan quickly escorted him out of the room.

Summer sat there, trying to decide how best to approach Brody and offer her sincerest apology. How to apologize for doubting him. How to apologize for being so quick to assume the worst. And how to tell him she still wanted to share her life with him. Thank God her ring was not at the bottom of the pool.

She knew how to reach Brody, but what she really wanted to do first was get in touch with Evan. She could not recall his private number, but she knew she could reach him, or at least get a message to him, through the record label.

"Music City Records," a perky receptionist answered. "How may I direct your call?

"I need to get a message to Evan. This is Summer Reynolds, and—"

The receptionist gasped. "I'm transferring you now to his private cell."

Evan answered on the first ring, as he had advised everyone at the record label that the only person they were to put through to his private cell was Summer. Still, he said a quick prayer before he answered. "Summer?"

"Evan!" She started to cry. "I'm so, so sorry for this awful misunderstanding. How can Brody possibly still want me in his life after I jumped to all the wrong conclusions? He's already married to me." It was hard for her to breathe. She felt like she was ready to collapse.

"Summer, he was beside himself when he couldn't find you. He was so intent on getting to Chicago to pick up Dr. Hunt that he realized he hadn't called you to tell you what was happening with Katie and the baby. So, trust me when I say the only person he is blaming in all this is himself."

"What can I do? Is he on his way to my house? Does he even know I'm at my parents' house? Can you give him my new phone number? I can't wait another moment to tell him I want to spend my life with him."

"Can you wait a couple of hours? I know it's a lot to ask, but I have an idea. There's only one problem, and you may not agree to it, because it would mean the world would then know who Brody is engaged to."

"I want the world to know he's engaged to me, especially after what we've both been through."

"I'll send one of the label's private planes for you. It should be there in a couple of hours. Can you be ready?"

"Yes, but what's your idea?"

"Before all this blew up, he was in the process of filming the music video for 'Summer Love.' He wanted to have you in the video but was certain you would not want to be recognized. We found someone who resembles you slightly, and at the end of the video, Brody gets down on one knee and proposes. I want you to be in the video, but I don't want Brody to know it's you until the end."

"I'll do it."

"Do you think your family will be on board with this? Yours is not the only life that is going to change dramatically once the video airs. I can probably get the network to hold off for an extra week or two before they release it, but that might be difficult. The fans were clamoring for this video even before he announced his retirement."

"Yes, about that ..."

"Summer, that is between you and Brody. I will accept whatever decision the two of you make."

Summer had never envisioned that one day she would be in one of Brody's music videos, even though she knew that other male artists sometimes had their wife appear in one. And she fervently hoped that she would be able to stay out of sight until just the right moment.

It was a frantic rush to get to the set. Autumn and her parents had chosen to stay behind, knowing that this was a private moment even though the cameras would be rolling. They were more supportive than Summer felt she had a right to expect.

Summer had never been behind the scenes of the making of a music video, and she found the whole process fascinating and surprising. But more than anything, she was nervous.

The actress who had been playing the role of Summer, Hope, was already there in place, so Brody would be expecting to see her as the music faded. Summer stayed out of sight with Evan.

"You realize, don't you, that you're going to have to shoot the ending over again? I doubt he'll stick to the script once he sees me."

Evan disagreed. "I think the ending will be perfect."

There was to have been a traditional-looking diamond engagement ring in the box. When Summer stepped forward, she was wearing Hope's wardrobe. Brody did not look up until he opened the box and saw Summer's sparkling emerald engagement ring. When he glanced up and saw her, everyone stopped dead in their tracks except for the cameramen, who somehow remembered to keep filming so the magic of the moment would be immortalized forever.

Brody managed to find his voice after a moment, took Summer's left hand, and said quietly, "My Summer love, will you marry me?"

Whatever Hope's lines were to have been were completely unnecessary. Summer nodded, and Brody slipped the ring on her finger and kissed her with so much passion and intensity that Evan had them stop filming. This was a private moment, one not meant for the world to see.

When he finally dragged his lips from hers, he took her into his dressing room. "How did this happen?" He wrapped her tightly in his arms. "How did you get here?"

"Evan."

Brody was trembling. "Thank God you're here. I thought I'd lost you—I thought I'd never see you again. I thought—"

"It doesn't matter what you thought, but I am so terribly sorry for what I thought. I thought I wasn't enough for you. I thought you loved me but didn't want to make love to me. I thought every time we were together and close to being intimate, you were thinking about another woman."

"I thought you didn't want a life in the spotlight."

She raised her head and looked deep into his eyes. "Was that your reason behind the press conference? Because if you're ready to stop recording and stop touring, that's one thing. But if you're only doing it because it's the only way you thought I would come back to you, you're wrong."

"You do know now that you're in the video that we won't be able to keep your identity a secret much longer, right?"

"When will it air?"

"They have to finish editing it. Normally from the time a video is filmed, it's about four to six weeks before it airs. Sometimes when awards nominations are right around the corner, they try to speed things up."

"So, we have some time to make plans."

"The Grand Hotel will be opening in mid-May. If you still want to get married there, we could probably convince them to let us get married a day or two before they are fully open for the season."

"I'd marry you tomorrow in your backyard."

"I know you would. But this is going to be my only wedding and your only wedding, and I want it to be perfect and beautiful and romantic. Since none of Antonio's designs wowed you, I want to fly you and your mother to Paris to buy your gown. I want the finest chef in the world flown in to make our wedding cake. We'll dance to our song, and then I will whisk you away to the honeymoon suite and we'll make a baby. But more than anything, I just want to be your husband."

"And I just want to be your wife, but you do not need to fly me to Paris to find a gown."

His voice suddenly turned serious and he whispered, "I have a confession to make."

"You can tell me anything. I don't want to ever go through anything like this again. I know in my heart how you feel about me, even though you've been reluctant to demonstrate it physically."

"I blame myself entirely for what happened."

"But why?"

"I was mad at myself for all the things I should have said and done. You value your virginity, and so do I. You will never know what it means to me to know that you saved yourself for me. But I saw the look in your eyes the last time I told you we needed to stop before things went too far. I knew if I had made love to you, if you had given yourself to me completely, you would have known I would never have taken that gift from you unless I was one hundred percent serious about our commitment. I know you have had doubts about how I could want you to the exclusion of all others. I never want you to doubt that, or me, again.

"I won't."

"I want you to understand what I'm saying. When we leave here, we are going to my house, and I am going to make love to you. And I know you might not be ready to move in with me, but I want to spend every day between now and the wedding with you."

She gave him just a hint of a smile. "Great minds think alike. I resigned from my job and gave my landlord notice. I am ready to start our life together right here, right now."

"And your family? What will they think? I don't want to drive a wedge between you. Do you think they would feel better if they knew we had already said vows to one another?"

"My mother would be devastated, and my father would never get over not being there to walk me down the aisle the first time ... so no. That needs to stay between us, now and forever."

"Forever. I like the sound of that."

"And I like the sound of a May wedding at the Grand Hotel. So, we better get to work."

"And we will! But first, the current and future Mrs. Martin, I need to show you how I feel about you." He picked her up effortlessly in his arms and carried her out of the studio, to the delight of everyone there.

"I still have the wardrobe on!" she protested.

"And I'll make sure someone sends your clothes to the house." He leaned closer to whisper in her ear, "Not that you will be wearing anything for very long."

They departed to laughter, more than a few tears, and thunderous clapping from the crew members.

"Carl's waiting for us. Let me take you home."

The excitement of the day had worn Summer out, and she fell asleep in the back of the limo on the way to Brody's house. She was having a sensuous, erotic dream, and when she woke up, Brody's hands were weaving a delicious trail down her body. "I can't wait to touch you," he whispered.

"How close are we to the house?"

Brody took a quick glance outside. "Maybe ten minutes or so. Why?"

She started to unzip his slacks when he stopped her. "My love, our first time is not going to be in the back of a limo. There's going to be wine and candles and music. I want to lay on the bed and watch you take off all your clothes. I want to kiss you everywhere from the top of your head to your sweet little toes. I want to make you come with my mouth. And then I want to possess you, body and soul."

"Brody ..." Her body was quivering with nerves and anticipation. "What if I don't ... satisfy you?"

He could tell from the look in her eyes that she was deadly serious. "Trust me, that is one thing you do *not* need to worry about."

"There are times when I almost wish I had some experience."

"I'm not sure I've ever really described to you how I feel about being your first."

"And my last," she reminded him.

"Yes. And even though we both know you will not be my first, trust me when I say this: Making love to you is going to be different from anything I have experienced before. I have never felt such a deep connection to someone. The only thing I'm worried about is overwhelming you. I don't want to hurt you or do anything to make you uncomfortable, so you need to be able to tell me what you like, and what you don't like."

She tried to imagine verbalizing that when they were in the throes of passion. "All I can say is that I promise to try. At this point, I don't even know what I'm going to like or not like."

He kissed her sweetly and tried to put her mind at ease. "When the time comes, I promise, you'll know."

Chapter Nineteen

꧁

When they arrived at the house, neither one of them spoke to Carl, instead racing to the front door like their clothes were on fire. Brody unlocked the door and swept her up into his arms for the second time that afternoon. "I know this is a bit premature, but I want to carry you over the threshold. I'll do it again after our official wedding, but in my mind and in my heart, this is our wedding night." He carried her up the stairs as he raced to their bedroom.

"Who did all this? You weren't kidding about the wine and the candles and the music, but you neglected to tell me about the rose petals!"

"Evan put Mandy to work as soon as you agreed to play yourself in the music video. Which, by the way, was the best surprise of my life."

She tingled with excitement. "Are you going to seduce me?"

"Do you want to be seduced?"

"I do. I want you to take me and make me yours."

"You have no idea how many nights I laid in my bed, or a hotel bed, after we had talked on the phone and fantasized about what it would be like the first time." He closed the door behind them, and she raised her eyebrows when he locked it.

"I'm not expecting any interruptions … but I'm also not taking any chances."

"And it will be a good thing to get into the habit of doing once the babies arrive."

"I'm ready for you to take your clothes off," he reminded her.

"I think I'd like it better if you undressed me, Brody. I want your hands all over me."

He slowly unbuttoned the flowered sundress she was wearing. "This never looked as good on Hope as it looks on you."

"The bodice is a little tight."

"That's because you fill it out so nicely."

She shimmied out of the dress and stood before him in lace skimpy enough to make his blood boil. Her bra barely contained her generous breasts. With one flick of his hand, he had unclasped it and bent down to take one nipple in his mouth, and then the other. When he raised his head to kiss her, she whispered in his ear, "My panties are wet."

"And to think you were worried about this," he couldn't help but tease her. "Somehow, you instinctively know all the right things to say to turn me on." He slid a hand inside her panties to discover that she was already slick with desire. When he bent to remove them, he pressed a kiss to the juncture of her thigh. "Lay down on the bed, and let me make love to my wife."

"Before you do that, there's something you need to know."

The uncertainty in her voice unnerved him. If she had decided she wanted to wait until their actual wedding night, he could deal with that, but this seemed like something far more serious.

She hesitated before she continued, and that made him even more nervous. "A couple of weeks before Christmas, I decided to go to the doctor and have an examination."

Later, Brody would say he swore his heart stopped in that moment. Was she sick? Did she have an incurable disease? Was she dying? Would the life he had planned for them never come to reality?

He turned pale, and she was quick to reassure him everything was okay. "Brody, I didn't mean to scare you! I had my doctor write me a prescription for birth control pills. He said I should wait a full two months to make sure they were effective before I had unprotected sex."

"So, it's safe? You're safe?" He started to babble, which she found endearing. "I'm safe. I had my doctor check me out right after we met."

"We're safe." She moved closer and felt his erection pressed against her. "And ..."

"And?"

"Don't make me wait another minute." She lay down on the bed and pulled him down with her. She caressed his erection and said, "I want to feel you inside me."

He knew the lubricated condoms he had purchased would have made things easier for her the first time, but he was as anxious as she was to be inside her with nothing between them.

She closed her eyes in anticipation of feeling him enter her, but she was surprised when he nudged her legs apart and found her center with his mouth. It was unexpected, and when she opened her eyes to watch him licking her, she started to squirm beneath him.

He stopped momentarily, unsure as to what her movements meant. "Stop?"

She shook her head vigorously from side to side. "Don't stop," she panted, straining against something just out of reach. When he plundered her with his fingers as he continued to circle her with his tongue, she let all her inhibitions go. "I feel like I'm coming apart from the inside out!" she screamed as he continued to lick her until the spasms finally stopped.

While her body was still tingling with her first orgasm, he slid ever so slowly into her, wanting to enter her when her body was sensitive. "Does it hurt?"

"I didn't think it was possible to feel both pleasure and pain simultaneously."

"Pain? Do you want me to stop?"

"No. More," she murmured. "I need more. I need all of you."

Before she knew what was happening, he had reversed their positions so she was on top. Her movements were instinctive, and the sensation of her riding him and the way her breasts bounced inched him ever closer to the edge. He wanted to make it last longer, but it seemed futile.

He started counting to a hundred. He thought about being audited by the IRS. He thought about having a root canal. But nothing could stop him from coming when she said, "Take me over the edge with you, Brody," sending them both reeling with simultaneous orgasms.

They drifted off to sleep wrapped in each other's arms. After round two, they took a shower and finally made their way downstairs, where a picnic dinner was waiting for them. When Summer took her last bite of fried chicken, she said, "Remind me to send a thank-you note to Mandy. She really did think of everything."

Brody looked behind her to the moonlight shimmering on the surface of the pool, and his eyes grew dark with desire. "What do you think about a moonlit dip in the pool?"

"Clothing optional?"

"Clothing optional."

Before he could put down his glass of sweet tea, she was out the sliding door, casting his T-shirt she'd borrowed aside and diving into the pool. He moved a little slower, and she beckoned him with her finger. Her breasts were barely peeking out of the water and he hardened instantly. "I see you're ready for round three. Come make love to me while the water swirls around us." He was only too happy to comply.

If Summer's parents were unhappy with her decision to stay with him until the wedding, they did not voice their concerns, and she spoke with both them and Autumn regularly.

The next days and weeks passed in a blur of lovemaking, overseeing the completion of the library and the recording studio, and finalizing their wedding plans.

One day, reality intruded when Evan called to inform them the music network was planning the world premiere of the video for "Summer Love" that weekend. There were lengthy discussions back and forth and, in the end, Brody decided he wanted to hold a press conference before the video aired. Summer was insistent she be there by his side. Evan agreed, but Brody was reluctant. "Are you sure you want to do this after the whole Katie fiasco?"

"The whole Katie fiasco, as you described it, is exactly why I want to do this. There will be a lot less speculation about everything if I'm by your side."

Brody made the necessary arrangements, and Summer called her parents and siblings to advise them to be prepared for the publicity.

On the way to the studio, Brody made one last attempt to get her to change her mind. "I'm a little worried that you haven't found a dress yet. Aren't you worried? Because if you're not worried, I'm worried that *you're* not worried. And now it's going to be even harder to go into a bridal shop unrecognized!"

She patted his arm affectionately. "It's all under control."

"Well, if it suddenly spirals out of control, my offer to fly you and your mother to Paris still stands."

"And a very generous offer, it is. But do I strike you as the kind of girl who wants to buy her wedding gown in Paris?"

"No," he admitted. "And that's one of the things I love the most about you. You don't care about my wealth or my planes or my cars."

The press conference had drawn a lot of curiosity and speculation, and the general consensus was that he was going to recant on his decision to retire. In spite of the fact that he had announced that he was in love at his last press conference, the reporters were wholly unprepared to see him walk onto the podium holding the hand of a woman no one recognized.

"I'll make this short and sweet. Today, I am here to announce my engagement to this beautiful woman standing next to me." He kissed her left hand, then held it up so her ring was on display for everyone to see. The applause was deafening. "She is the star of my new music video and the inspiration for the song 'Summer Love.'"

The barrage of questions began, and Brody singled out some reporters who he had a positive relationship with.

"Have you set a date?"

"We have" was all he replied.

"Have you chosen a location?"

"Yes," he laughed good-naturedly, "but my future in-laws would have my head on a platter if I told you any of the details."

"Are you still planning to retire?"

"My summer tour is back on." That declaration was met with more applause. "But that is all I'm willing to commit to for the moment."

The questions continued, but Evan announced that was all for the day. With that, Summer and Brody made their escape to where Carl was waiting in a limo.

"That wasn't so bad for my first time," Summer murmured.

"I agree. And, by the way, I have enjoyed *all* our firsts. The first time I made you come with my mouth and you screamed. The first time I claimed you with my body. The first time we made love in the shower, and in the pool, and in the library, and in the recording studio, and in the gazebo …"

"And in the limo."

"We haven't made love in the limo."

"Not yet, but we're about to."

Chapter Twenty

ॐ

Before they knew it, it was time for their families to assemble at the Grand Hotel for the wedding festivities. Besides family, there were only a few close friends in attendance, including Evan and Carl and their better halves.

Several of Summer's closest friends were there, too, as well as Katie and her husband. The children had accompanied them along with a nanny that Brody had hired.

The rehearsal went smoothly, and everyone attended the rehearsal dinner afterwards. The food, wine, and conversation flowed effortlessly. Brody and Summer never ceased to be amazed at how well their families got along.

As dinner was winding down, Brody announced that it was time to give his bride her gift. There was much teasing about everything he had already given her—the Corvette, the library, and even a scholarship he had endowed at her college for future students who wanted to pursue a career in writing.

He raised a glass to toast her. "One of the things I learned about Summer very early on is that she is as close to her family as I am to mine. They have instilled in her many of the same values that my family taught me. So, when I learned that the property adjacent to mine was about to be listed for sale, I had Evan make the owners an offer they could not refuse. There are actually two separate residences on the property." He pulled two keys from his jacket pocket, handing one to his parents and one to Summer's. "Now, you will each have a place of your own when you come to visit."

This came as a complete surprise to Lynn, Mitch, Leslie, and Scott, but no one was more pleased than Summer.

Summer raised her glass to toast her groom. "I have a special gift for Brody, too ... but I want to give it to him in private." Her announcement was followed by a lot of good-natured teasing as they departed, hand in hand.

Summer had insisted they stay in separate accommodations, saying that Brody was not to see her on the morning of the wedding. But when they reached her cottage, he was looking at her like he was still hungry and she was his second dessert.

"It this gift, by any chance, a racy, lacy, tiny little scrap of something in red?"

"For someone who removes my lingerie about thirty seconds after I put it on, you certainly have a fondness for it—but no. And in case you have any thoughts about spending the night with me, there will be no hanky-panky tonight."

"What if I told you I had big plans?"

"Trust me, I know how big your ... *plans* are."

She reached down to take a box off her dresser and handed it to him. "Your gift was unbelievable. How many men would want his in-laws living next door, even if it isn't year-round?"

"You forget, *your* in-laws will also be next door." He began shaking his box like a kid on Christmas morning, speculating about its contents. "Too heavy to be lingerie. Keys to a Ferrari? A gift certificate for a hot air balloon ride?"

"Will you just get on with it already?" The minute she saw the gleam in his eyes, she knew that was the wrong thing to have said. "I mean, unwrap your present."

"I'd rather unwrap you, but here goes."

She had purposely packaged it in a large box so as to better disguise what it was. When he opened the box, his eyes could not hide his surprise and his pleasure.

"It's an advance copy. Lillian made the arrangements for me to have it before we left on our honeymoon."

He held the book in his hands with reverence, and when he read the title, his voice was thick with emotion. "*The Magical Unicorn* by Summer Martin." He turned to the first page and got choked up by the simple but heartfelt dedication. "'For Brody, who taught me to believe in fairy tales and magical unicorns.'"

She leaned up to wipe a stray tear from his eyes. "It's the first in a series. It should be in production and in books stores in about three months."

He finally found his voice. "So, my wife is going to be a published author. Were you working on this when I was finishing my album?" He put the book down gently and wrapped her in his arms. "I am so unbelievably proud of you. Do your parents know about this? Autumn?"

"I wanted you to be the first one to know. I never in a million years thought anyone would want to publish it. It started out as a nice little story I thought I could read to our children someday."

His eyes travelled over every inch of her body, thinking about planting his seed and watching it grow. He knew her curves like the back of his hand. He still could not believe this gorgeous creature, who had the biggest heart of anyone he knew, had fallen in love with him. "So ... you were serious about no hanky-panky tonight?"

"I was. But wait right there for a minute. I want to do something symbolic tonight, the last night before I can officially call myself Mrs. Brody Martin."

He was at a loss as to what she had planned now, still reeling from the unexpected surprise of *The Magical Unicorn*.

Summer returned from the bathroom with her birth control pills in her hand. "We don't need these anymore." She pushed each one out of the foil and into the nearest waste basket. "We can start making our family tomorrow night."

"Are you sure we don't need to practice? I have something you could unwrap," he said as he placed her hand on the bulge in his slacks.

"Save it for our wedding night, big boy."

He reluctantly left her side, but not before cupping her face with his hands and kissing her first sweetly, and then with all the fire and passion in his soul. If he was going to go to bed sexually frustrated, he wanted to make sure she would be, too.

"I'll be counting the hours until I see you walking down the garden path tomorrow. I know you will be gorgeous, even though I haven't a clue what your dress looks like."

"And you're not supposed to know. Now go, before I change my mind."

Sleep was almost impossible for Summer that night, and she suspected that it was for Brody as well. All their dreams were about to come true, and she hoped with all her heart that it would not be long before her dream of giving him a child also came true.

Their wedding day dawned sunny and clear, every bit as perfect as Summer had dreamed. She thought back to her life the previous spring. She'd had a nice life, although a bit ordinary. She would never have predicted falling in love with a superstar, or ever in her wildest dreams thought that he would love her in equal measure. Over the years she had listened to Brody's music, watched his videos, seen him accept awards, and dreamed about one day meeting him—getting his autograph, maybe posing for a picture with him. But today, they would be posing for their wedding pictures that would go on to be published in countless magazines.

Leslie and Lynn had planned a lovely brunch for Summer. As the girls shared mimosas and memories, Summer nibbled at her food, starting to feel nervous for the first time. "I'm beginning to wish we had planned a morning ceremony. Why did I think a late afternoon wedding was a good idea?"

"Well," Lynn said, "your mother and I thought you might need something to occupy some of your time, so we booked a tour of the hotel and some of the filming locations from the movie. The tour begins in about twenty minutes."

The time passed more quickly than Summer expected, and soon enough it was time to get ready. Brody had sent her random sweet texts throughout the day, reminding her of some of the special moments they had shared.

After being nervous all morning, she was suddenly calm and composed, and she imagined that Brody was too. But when Cassidy came back from checking on Brody and the groomsmen, she was laughing. "I wish you could see Brody! He said he's more nervous than the first time he was up for a big award. I know you don't want to see him before the ceremony, but it might not be a bad idea to call him."

He answered on the first ring in a frantic voice, "What is it? What's wrong? Did you change your mind? You can tell me anything as long as it's not goodbye."

"I wanted to make sure *you* didn't change your mind! You're stuck with me. There will never be another man I give my heart and my body to. I am going to go on wanting you and needing you and loving you for the rest of my life."

"You are the first thing I want to see each morning when I open my eyes, and the last thing I want to see each night when I close them."

"The sooner we hang up, the sooner we can take the walk that will change our lives."

Until it was time to walk down the aisle, they were both lost in their own thoughts. Brody had fretted about Summer having difficulty finding a wedding gown, and the truth was he had no idea just how perfect her wedding gown was.

Summer was relieved that they had already made love, so she wasn't a bundle of nerves. worrying about pleasing him. She was also more than ready to make a baby. She hadn't been entirely kidding when she said she wanted five. Or maybe six? A nice even number.

Soon Summer's father arrived to escort her down the garden path, his eyes filled with tears, everyone moved to give them a moment alone.

"I've never seen a more beautiful bride, except for your mother. "

"Thank you, Daddy." For a moment, she sounded just like his little girl again.

"I couldn't ever give you away if I didn't know in my heart that you and Brody are meant for one another." He kissed her forehead tenderly.

"As much as I love your sister and your brothers, you and I have always shared a special bond. And I hope that someday, you and Brody are blessed with a daughter as sweet and special as you are. I thought the day I would give you away was further into the future, but I know that Brody is your destiny. So … let's get this show on the road!"

Chapter Twenty-One

🐋

The gardens were a beautiful riot of colors and scents. Butterflies flitted gracefully from stem to stem, and the air held a mixture of romance and excitement.

As Brody stood anxiously by the minister, he thought he was prepared for his first glimpse of his bride, but he could not have been more mistaken. Of all the wedding gowns in the world, he had never expected to see her gliding toward him in his grandmother Lucia's.

After her father kissed Summer's cheek and put her hand in Brody's, he whispered, "Take good care of my girl."

Brody was mesmerized, already speechless when Summer leaned toward him and whispered, "I know she is here with us today. I want to name our first daughter after her."

He could not resist the urge to lean in and kiss her on the lips, to everyone's delight.

They had written their own vows, and as Brody started to speak, silent tears began to stream down Summer's cheeks. It had been seven months since their secret ceremony, but here in front of all their loved ones he repeated his first vows to her, word for word.

"I bought your engagement ring the day after I met you. I flew to New York City and convinced Tiffany's to open early for me." He heard both of their mothers gasp before he continued. "I never thought I would give it to you as soon as I did, but I knew it was meant to be yours, just as I am. I want to be your friend, your love, your lover, your husband, the father of your children. You and I both know you are not the first woman I have loved, but you have my solemn vow that you will be the last." He lifted her hand and kissed her ring, and she began to speak.

"Our crazy whirlwind love affair is like something out of a romance novel. Believing in love at first sight was just a fantasy to me until the first time our eyes met. I knew I had found the one—the other half of my heart, the one who would laugh with me, cry with me, and support me through good times and in bad. I know you're not perfect"—the guests all heard his parents chuckle at that—"but you're perfect for me."

When the minister announced them husband and wife, they sealed it with a kiss that went on for so long, Summer became dizzy as everyone clapped and cheered.

The reception was lovely, every detail arranged exactly the way they wanted, but all Brody and Summer could think about was the next phase of the evening. Even though they had made love hundreds of times in different ways, they knew that this night would be more special than all the ones that had come before.

When it was time for the bridal dance, Brody pulled her close and the music started. She looked up at him with questioning eyes. "Why aren't we dancing to 'Summer Love'?"

"Just be quiet, my love, and listen." The background music gave way to Brody's rich baritone singing a brand-new song she had never heard before. As the chorus came and Brody sang the title, "Lifetime Love," she was instantly transported back to the moment when she had given him the idea for it.

"It's beautiful."

"This song is meant to be shared with only my lovely bride and our friends and families. I will never release this, or sing it live. But as beautiful as the song is, it is not as beautiful as you."

"You're the first man to make me feel beautiful," she confessed.

"They were all fools," he reassured her.

She shook her head. "I don't think it was just that. I couldn't give my heart to anyone else because this whole time, I was waiting for you."

When it was time for the bride and groom to depart, down at the bottom of the famous porch steps was a horse-drawn carriage. "I know I couldn't give you a normal wedding—the kind your friends will all have someday—but I'm glad I could give you a fairy-tale wedding fit for a princess."

She had already removed her veil, and Brody reached out to take something from Autumn. "And every princess needs one of these." The porch lights made the brilliant diamond tiara sparkle.

"Oh, Brody, you shouldn't have!" There as a collective sigh from all the women watching. "Are they ... real?"

"Yes, they are. And very old. I bought it at an online estate sale. I hope someday our daughter can wear it on her wedding day."

"And I hope I never wake up from this dream," she sighed as he held out her hand so she could step up into the carriage.

"We're going to take a little ride around the grounds before we head to our honeymoon cottage. Autumn packed up all your things, and Carl already has your bags for the honeymoon."

"Yes, and it was a little hard to pack for a month-long honeymoon when you won't give me any hints as to where we're going!"

"I'm sure we can buy whatever you might need along the way."

When they arrived at the cottage reserved for their wedding night, she was not surprised to find it filled with flickering candles and white roses. They walked outside to watch the stars for a moment before he took her in his arms. "As much as I love seeing you in my grandmother's wedding gown, it's time to take it off."

"I looked at gown after gown, and none of them were right. Then one night, your mother invited me over and told me she had been saving this for Bailey and Brennan, but they both thought it was a little old-fashioned for their tastes and gave me their blessing to wear it."

"It suits you perfectly." Brody's hands were trembling as he tried to undo all the impossibly tiny white buttons that ran down the back of the gown. "And you looked like a princess even without the tiara."

"That was a bit over-the-top, don't you think?"

"It was. But admit it, you loved it."

"Yes, I did." The gown slipped from her shoulders to reveal she was wearing the sexiest bra and tiniest thong he had ever seen her wear. "You're such a contradiction," he growled with passion. "Demure on the outside and a sex goddess in the bedroom."

"And you are wearing far too many clothes, Mr. Martin." He shed his tuxedo jacket and she went to work unbuttoning his shirt, kissing his golden chest until she reached the waist of his pants and slipped her hand inside. "Time to do what I didn't do last night." He hadn't even had time to step out of his slacks when she took his engorged penis in her mouth.

"Summer, I want to come inside you."

She stopped only long enough to say, "Oh, you will," and seconds later, she stopped when he was right on the edge.

He removed her bra and panties and reached for the tiara that she had set down. "I want you to wear this while I ravish you." He pushed her down on the bed and filled her in one swift stroke. "But I'm just warning you, I won't be able to last long. You're so tight and wet, and when you clench around me, I want to pump everything I have into you. You were made for me."

"And you were made for me."

He continued to slide slowly in and out of her until she grasped his butt and pulled him as far in as he would go, talking dirty to him the whole time until both their worlds collided.

"Do you think it will always be like this?" she asked softly.

"Like what?" he teased, knowing full well what she meant.

"Wonderful. Prefect. You make me tingle in places I didn't know could tingle."

After more lovemaking, and very little sleep, morning arrived. They looked at each other with sleepy, satisfied eyes. "Now, Mrs. Martin, we can finally be seen together in public holding hands and wearing our wedding bands." He reached into her robe to tease one nipple into tight perfection. "Let's go take a shower. Carl won't be here for another hour and a half."

Showering together and another round of lovemaking took up most of those ninety minutes. When Summer started to fret, Brody placed a finger over her lips. "Don't worry. It's not like my plane can leave without us."

When Carl called to say he had arrived, Summer suddenly asked, "How are we getting to the airport? Your plane couldn't land on the island."

"Carl is also a licensed helicopter pilot. He's flying us to the lower peninsula, where the plane is waiting."

Thankfully the ride was both short and smooth, and Summer felt no signs of motion sickness. When they flew over the lighthouse, Summer remarked that that was one of her mother's favorite sights.

"My favorite sight was seeing you walk toward me in my grandmother's wedding gown. I was floored."

"So was I when your mother offered it to me." In all the pre-wedding and wedding excitement, Summer had completely forgotten that the gown was not the only thing she had from his grandmother. She had meant to give it to him last night until passion took over and they couldn't keep their hands off one another.

"I wish you could have met her. She would have loved you."

When they boarded the plane, Summer looked at him intently. "Time to tell me where we're going. All you said was to pack a mixture of casual and classy. So, I have to ask, where are we headed?"

"I'll give you a hint as to our first destination. What is one of the most romantic locations you can think of?"

"Anywhere you are."

"Good answer, but not the one I was looking for."

"Paris—no, Venice."

He acted surprised by her response when, in fact, he had quizzed her parents and Autumn to get an idea as to what European destinations she might be the most excited to see. "What a coincidence—those are two of the stops on our honeymoon tour. I want to take you to the top of the

Eiffel Tower and on a gondola ride in Venice and to England to see the Crown Jewels. Anywhere and everywhere your heart desires."

When they reached cruising altitude, Brody was ready to pop open a bottle of champagne and chocolate-covered strawberries when she abruptly stopped him. "Anywhere and everywhere my heart desires?" He nodded his agreement, and she took him by the hand. "Then take me to bed, Brody."

He put the champagne and strawberries back in the frig and when he reached the bedroom he was stunned by the sight of her wearing nothing but his cowboy hat and a smile "I found something interesting in the refrigerator in here."

She held out a can of whipped cream and told him to strip. When he stood naked before her, she covered his throbbing shaft with whipped cream and dropped to her knees. "I want to lick you until you come." It was only moments until he shot into her mouth and took the can from her.

"Two can play at this game," he said as he pushed her back onto the bed. "I want to lick you from head to toe, but mostly somewhere in between." He knew all her erogenous zones, and exactly what made her scream. He knew from the way her breathing changed when she was close to coming. He knew she liked it when he slid into her right when she was still convulsing from her first orgasm. She was the perfect woman who commanded his attention both in and out of the bedroom.

As soon as his mouth landed on her right breast, she grasped his head, urging him to hurry up. "Get to the good parts," she whimpered.

"You mean like these parts?" His fingers traced a trail of whipped cream down her body. "I guess I will have to lick my way down to the good parts." He proceeded to do just that as she writhed beneath him, inching ever so close to coming when he would stop and use his tongue on a different part of her body. "Brody, you're driving me slowly crazy."

"Would it help if I told you I'm ready to slide inside you so we can drive each other crazy?"

She looked down to discover that he was, once again, ready to take her to new heights of passion.

Once they were both exhausted and satisfied she looked at him with a serious expression.

"What, my wife?"

"I can't believe out of all the women in the world you chose me."

"And I can't believe you chose to save yourself for me. I can't wait to show you all the romantic places in Europe, places, I want you to know, that I have never taken anyone else."

Their European honeymoon was like something out of every woman's fantasy, sightseeing by day and making hot, passionate love at night. One of the unexpected bonuses was that most European fans were more respectful and better at keeping their distance than their counterparts in the States. There were a few requests for photographs and autographs, but not many. Every day had been better than the one before, but they were both ready to go home and begin their new married life.

"The fans here have been wonderful. You should really think about doing a European tour before you hang up your cowboy hat."

"Darlin', that hat looks a lot better on you than it does on me." He leaned over to whisper in her ear, "Especially when that's all you're wearing."

"You certainly know how to say all the right things."

"And I mean every one of them. I can't promise you that every day will be wine and roses, but I will love you until the day I die. I saw the way my grandfather treated my grandmother, the way he courted her every day of their life, and I make the same promise to you."

Chapter Twenty-Two

❦

everal weeks after they returned home, Summer started to feel tired and moody. She wanted to confirm her suspicions before Brody started to suspect something, but it helped that Autumn had come for a visit and was feeling under the weather when she left. *I could just be sick with something*, Summer thought.

Katie and her family had recently moved to the area, and her husband had gone to work for Brody's record label. The foursome had bonded after the birth and recovery of Allison. So, since Summer did not want to get in touch with her mother in case she just had a bug after all, she called Katie.

"Are you up for company? I feel like taking the Corvette out for a spin, and I would love to see you and the girls."

"Of course! I'd love to show you the new house, and Talia and Allison would love to see their Aunt Summer. Will Brody be joining us?"

"He's working on new music, so it'll just be us girls."

Summer was afraid of going into a drugstore to buy a pregnancy kit and getting recognized, but Katie was thrilled to do it. She left Summer with the girls while she ran out to pick one up.

When she returned, she peppered Summer with question after question from the other side of the bathroom door. "Are you excited? Nervous? Was this planned, unplanned?"

Summer hadn't answered yet when she opened the door in shock and disbelief. "It's positive! I'm going to have Brody's baby!"

"Before you get too excited, take another one—I bought two. We want to make sure it's not a false positive."

The bathroom door closed again, and when Summer opened it, she nodded excitedly. "What now? I'm scared and thrilled and nauseous. I want to cry and scream and laugh and jump for joy!"

"Welcome to motherhood. I know you have a local doctor. Is it a family practice?"

"Yes, I guess I need to call and make an appointment. I'm still a bit shell-shocked. Looking back, I realize I should have had my period in Venice, but with all the traveling and sightseeing, I guess I never gave it much thought."

"But happy?" Katie looked a little worried.

"Not just happy. *Ecstatic.* I just wasn't sure it would happen as quickly as it did."

"Any idea how far along you are?"

"No. I threw out my birth control pills the night before the wedding. Brody is going to be over the moon."

"Just a word of caution … I'd wait until the doctor confirms it before you tell him."

"That makes sense. I just hope they can fit me in soon. I won't be able to hide this from him."

Hurriedly calling her doctor, she was relieved to hear they had a cancellation for the following afternoon. "Thank God! I'm no good at keeping secrets. I'll just have to tell him later that I'm not feeling well and hope he accepts it at face value."

That evening she ate lightly, pleaded a headache and sore throat, and complained about her sister and her germs. "You go on tour in three weeks. I hope you don't come down with this."

If he was suspicious, he didn't let on. He made her a cup of tea with honey, poured her a bath, and reluctantly agreed to let her sleep in one of the guest bedrooms.

The following afternoon, Brody had a meeting with Evan, so she was able to slip out of the house to her doctor appointment without having to explain where she was going. A little after three o'clock, the test results were confirmed, and her due date was Brody's birthday. She had spent a restless night trying to decide how best to share the news with him when she suddenly landed on the perfect idea.

She planned a romantic dinner for two and his favorite dessert, and on her way home she picked up everything she would need. Later that night when the meal was over, he pulled her onto his lap. "I'm glad you're feeling better. It was hard to leave you alone last night."

"And I see it's getting hard now."

"You're intoxicating," he said as he brushed a strand of her hair aside so he could nibble on her neck. "We didn't even have any wine with dinner and I feel like I'm drunk on love. Let's turn in early."

"Before we head to the bedroom, I have a letter for you to read."

"You wrote me a love letter?"

"I didn't, but someone who loved you did." She handed him a fragile letter, brittle with age. "When we unpacked your grandmother's wedding gown, we found this letter she wrote to you on your sixteenth birthday." Her eyes flooded with tears as her voice became thick with emotion.

"Did you read it?" His eyes were full as well.

"No, but I'd like it if you read it to me."

Together, they moved to the family room and sat down. "'My dearest Brody, one of my biggest regrets is that I will not live long enough to see you become a man. I hope someday, your amazing gift will take you to Nashville and beyond. I know in my heart that fame awaits you, and I also know you won't let it change you.'" He stopped reading, unable to continue. "Will you finish reading it?"

Summer's hands trembled as she took the letter from him. She was now so grateful that she had saved it for this special day, a day even more special than their wedding day.

"'Of all my grandchildren, you are my favorite. Our times in the kitchen are some of my fondest memories. You paid close attention to everything I taught you, both in and out of the kitchen. Someday, you will be making my sauce for your girlfriend.'" Now Summer was choked up. "'And someday, maybe she will be your wife. I hope when you find the other half of your heart, you never let her go. Your grandfather was the first and only man I loved, and he courted me every day. When you look into the eyes of your beloved, I hope you look at her the way he looked at me." Summer paused to wipe away her tears, not wanting to damage the delicate handwriting. "I hope you will choose a girl with old-fashioned values who will treat your heart with care and respect. Someday, when you marry her, I hope she wears this gown so I can be there with you."

He laid the letter gently beside him. "She was there with us that day," he said with great reverence. "I'm sure of it."

Summer took his hand and placed it on her stomach. "She's with us right now, Brody."

His eyes widened with hope. "What are you trying to tell me?"

"We're going to be parents. And if it's a girl, we are going to name her Lucia."

His love for her had never shone so brightly as it did in his eyes at that moment. He could not wait to see his child growing, feel him or her kick for the first time, pick out a crib and tiny outfits—he was excited for all of it.

They planned a dinner for their families, and everyone was excited when they announced the news. Autumn was pleased for her sister, but sad for reasons known only to her.

The shopping and planning began in earnest, and then at her first sonogram appointment, they discovered that they were not expecting one baby, but two.

There was a lot of conversation about whether or not they wanted to know the sex of the babies, but in the end they both decided they wanted to be surprised.

They waited until she was well into her second trimester before they announced their news together on *Music City Morning*. Soon thereafter, baby gifts starting arriving in droves at the record label. Most were donated to a local women's shelter, but they did receive one special gift from a newly married couple they had met one night during their honeymoon.

Summer read the short note that accompanied the gift. "They're ex-

pecting, too! Brody, we need to find something special to send them."
Brody was touched that his wife had kept in touch with the strangers
they had met one night on a rainy Paris street and counted them now
among their friends.

Right on cue, in the early morning hours of Brody's birthday, Summer went into labor and their families anxiously assembled at the hospital.

After what had seemed like endless hours of waiting, the doors
opened, and a beaming Brody walked out holding one pink bundle
and one blue. "I want you to meet Lucia and her brother Leo, short for
Leonard, named after my grandparents."

The twins consumed both their lives and their time, and it was wonderful to have two sets of grandparents close by. Their home was full
of love, laughter, diapers, and a new cat, Buffy, who they were quick to
point out had adopted them, not the other way around.

There was nothing in life Brody enjoyed more than singing lullabies
to his children every night and sleeping next to his Summer love, the
woman who had changed the course of his life. He knew in his heart
that somehow, someway, Lucia had sent her to him.

Printed in the USA
CPSIA information can be obtained
at www.ICGtesting.com
LVHW031916101123
763491LV00035B/1698/J

9 781959 677826